PURSE DOG RESCUE

---

*CUPID HAS
FOUR LEGS*

PURSE DOG RESCUE

ERIN L. JUNGDAHL

To Dallas, the first Chihuahua I ever loved.

Chapter One

ODIE

A golden retriever ruined my day. Not that it was great to start—the spring of two thousand eleven was shaping up to be the hottest I'd ever suffered living in Los Angeles. The humidity made my hair frizz around my temples and out of its ponytail, while the sweat running down my back turned my turquoise shirt an even soggier shade of blue. Still, my discomfort was nothing compared to that of poor old Diego. The fat black senior Chihuahua I was walking wheezed and carried on like he was going to collapse from heat exhaustion. I don't know what I was thinking when I dragged him and a pair of tiny fluffy dogs on a walk with Carmencita. The heat didn't seem to bother her as she stopped once a minute to sniff every unusually tall blade of grass before racing off to yap at anything with a shadow. It was lucky she was such an adorable tawny Chihuahua puppy, because her behavior on walks was anything but cute.

As we walked from the shelter to my favorite snow cone truck a few blocks away, we fell into a sort of rhythm in which Carmencita bounded ahead and half-dragged the three other dogs and me behind her. We would only slow down when Diego started wheezing and sputtering like his last breath was being rattled out of his pudgy little chest, but we would walk for just about a minute before blasting off again. After a few rounds, I thought I had a good handle on everything and every dog. This wasn't my first time walking multiple dogs—hell, it was part of my job. Possibly the best part of my job, or so I thought before we passed a giant golden retriever asleep under a restaurant patio umbrella.

All four dogs went ballistic. Diego was giving Carmencita a run for her money in terms of energetic and ferocious barking and growling. The golden retriever didn't crack open an eyelid, he just kept snoring while his companion, a bro with a soul patch and a plaid shirt, heaved an Oscar-worthy sigh. The impulse to roll my eyes was powerful, but the pull of gravity was stronger. Three leashes were wrapped around my legs as I fell hard on my ass. My ankle was twisted at an odd angle but my heart rose in my throat for an entirely different reason. Carmencita's leash was dragging along the ground as she sprinted toward the oblivious golden retriever. I flung myself forward only to scratch and burn my hands on the hot pavement.

A large tan hand grabbed the loop of Carmencita's leash and I felt a hand come to rest on my shoulder.

"Are you okay?"

I looked up and saw the most gorgeous man to ever walk the planet. He was all broad shoulders, glowing olive skin, wavy black hair, and warm brown eyes, and under any other circumstances I would have been blushing from the tips of my ears to the base of my throat. He was really that good-looking, and he seemed totally concerned about me. Finally, I found my words and blurted out, "I'll live, but these dogs might not."

There was low, smooth laughter coming from a nearby table, but Mr. Universe was determined to be my knight in shining armor. "You fell pretty hard on your ankle. Can you get up, or should we call somebody?"

I forced myself to press both hands to the cement and launch myself to my feet. I nearly toppled over, but my handsome rescuer steadied me with his well-muscled arms. I pushed away from him and smiled as I came to an uneasy standing pose. "I'm fine, see? I don't work far from here; I can make it back on my own."

Mr. Universe quirked an eyebrow. "Are you sure?"

"Oh, totally, but thanks for your help. Carmencita would have been flattened without you."

He looked down at the puppy at the end of the leash in his hands and smiled. God help me, he even had dimples! I nearly fainted from the sheer beauty standing in front of me with my most ridiculous shelter dogs. He shattered my reverie by dropping the leash in my hand. "But she gave me a great opportunity to talk to a beautiful woman. I'll remember Carmencita."

"If you know anyone looking to adopt a Chihuahua or another small dog, Carmencita and a few others are eagerly awaiting homes at the Purse Dog Rescue."

A light shined in Mr. Universe's eyes. He reached into his pocket and pulled a card out of his wallet, then placed the card on top of Carmencita's leash in my hands. "Call or text me to let me know that you made it home okay, please?"

I nodded, slipped the card into my dog-walking fanny pack, and turned to walk back to the shelter. I really wasn't in the mood for a snow cone anyway. Carmencita tried to stop and sniff every dandelion that grew between the cracks in the sidewalk, but my smarting ankle had worn my patience away to nothing. We left the fashionable cafés and boutiques behind us as we drew closer to the office park where I rented space for my baby, Purse Dog Rescue. Diego picked up the pace as we got closer. He was probably as excited by the prospect of air-conditioning as I was. When we came to the nondescript plate glass door on the side of the dingy white box that passed for professional real estate, I looped the dog leashes on one arm and pushed the door open.

At the front desk, Shereen didn't look up from her phone, the screen of which she was using as a mirror to apply thick brown lipgloss. I made a point to toss my fanny pack onto the chair next to my desk so that it made a loud squishy thud, but she couldn't be bothered to tear herself away from her afternoon grooming ritual. And to think I thought she might have been overqualified for a receptionist's gig when I hired her. Instead, Crystal, another employee and long-time friend, responded to our arrival with a curled lip and wrinkled forehead. "The hell happened to you?"

I limped past Crystal's desk, determined to put the dogs away before I got swept into explaining how an afternoon walk had gone so very wrong. Diego deserved to lie down anyway. I wasn't avoiding her, I was just doing my best by the dogs. But when we got to the back of the office with the giant kennels and I saw Diego's ears droop, guilt ripped through my heart. I needed to get after Shereen to do a social media blitz to find him a forever home. He wasn't cut out for life in a lonely kennel; he deserved so much better. The bonded pair of fluffy white dogs were totally indifferent to being taken off their leashes and left to their own devices in their stall—they were happy just to be with each other. Meanwhile, Carmencita started crying the second the gate to the kennel closed in front of her. She needed a foster home, and soon, if we were going to work on her less charming habits. Sure, she was a puppy, but badly behaved puppies were at risk of returning to the shelter. And I wouldn't wish that on any dog, not even a little punk like Carmencita.

Shereen was waiting by the door to the front office when I finished getting the dogs settled.

"Oh, sweetie! What happened to you? Your hair's a mess. Do you need to borrow some dry shampoo?"

I slumped into my desk chair and grimaced as the back of my sweaty shirt cemented to the pleather upholstery. "Thanks, Shereen. Could you grab an ice pack out of the freezer? Let me get my ankle sorted and then maybe we'll worry about my hair."

Shereen bounced off to the kitchen, and I leaned forward to examine my ankle. It had swollen considerably since I left the corner where I made a fool of myself in front of Mr. Universe.

Crystal rolled away from her desk to sit next to me. She stopped just short of knocking into me as she said, "You still haven't said what happened."

"I'll tell you when my ego's had a chance to recover." I sighed as Shereen plopped an ice pack wrapped in a dish towel in my hands.

Shereen stood in front of me for a minute, rocking on her right heel. "So I don't know if this is the right time to mention it, but I met the most amazing guy on Craigslist the other day. He's an Aries! Anyway, I was wondering if he could come with us on the winery tour. Can he come, please, Odie?"

Out of the corner of my eye, I could see Crystal vigorously shaking her head no and making a matching cutting motion with her arms. I scooted closer to my desk and drained my water bottle, which had left a damp ring on a stack of papers. Shereen was totally out of line asking to bring some random guy on an employee appreciation outing, but I hated—and I mean really hated—telling people no.

"So…what do you say?" Shereen prompted, flipping her balayage highlighted hair over her shoulders.

I could almost feel her staring down at me, but I couldn't bring myself to look up at her. The simple truth of the matter was that there was barely enough money to bring actual employees on the employee appreciation winery tour, much less plus-ones. All the same, I really, really, really hated to tell people no.

"Sure. I didn't budget for an extra person to come on the trip, but we can figure out a way. I just need you to double down on Diego's adoption campaign; he's killing me back there."

Crystal's curls bounced in the air as she threw her head in her hands.

Shereen wrapped me in a hug. "Thank you thank you thank you! You're the best boss ever! I can't wait to tell Brad."

She bounced over to her desk without acknowledging anything I said about Diego, and I sank further into my desk chair. I wanted more water but I absolutely did not want to get up. I could refill my bottle later, like when I was leaving the office to go visit my granny. But at that moment, I wasn't moving anywhere.

My computer made a dinging sound and I turned to investigate. Crystal had sent me an instant message.

Crystal Oglivy: Whhhhhhhhhy?

Me: It's an employee appreciation event. If it makes her feel more appreciated, then I'm happy to do it.

Crystal Oglivy: Where are you going to find the money to bring an extra person?

Me: I'll look through the books and find money somewhere.

Crystal Oglivy: If anyone should be bringing guests, it should be you. Namely, you should be bringing your grandmother. God knows she's donated enough to the Rescue.

Me: She knows it's just an employee thing.

Crystal Oglivy: Well, if your grandmother knows it's just an employee thing, shouldn't Shereen and her boy toy?

Me: I'm sorry, would you like me to rescind the invitation?

There was a pause and I saw Crystal's blue eyes narrowed in my direction. I shrugged my shoulders and picked my soggy shirt away from my back. My computer made another ding just as I started going through the planning spreadsheet for the winery tour.

Crystal Oglivy: No, you're the boss. But when you get a chance, we need to talk.

I turned to look at Crystal—she was packing up for the day. I glanced over at Shereen's desk and saw that she was already gone.

Before I could check the clock, Crystal spoke. "It's after five. Technically, she put in eight hours, if you consider her hour lunch break to be on the clock."

I snorted and started getting together the bag of things I always meant to work on at home but never got around to doing. It was purely wishful thinking that I would start working on a grant application for the Rescue off the clock. Never mind the fact that I usually helped Granny with her own projects in the evenings, but after three years of running the Rescue it was a habit. Crystal went to the back to feed the dogs for the night and let them outside to do their business.

When the dogs were put away, Crystal insisted on walking me to the door. My throbbing ankle made my teeth clench but I still managed to ask, "What was it you wanted to talk about?"

Crystal sighed. "I would talk now but I have a babysitting gig across town. Can we talk tomorrow, maybe go to lunch together or something?"

"You know I'm not going to sleep for wondering what you need to talk about, right?"

"It's nothing worth losing sleep over. Go home, rest your ankle, and say hello to Granny for me."

She walked out the door and I was left to lock up and limp to my used blue Prius by myself. I briefly thought of my dog-walking fanny pack I'd left inside, and Mr. Universe's card, but I couldn't bring myself to hear the dogs crying when I reopened the door only to close it again without saying goodbye. So I left.

Chapter Two

I watched Victor's damsel-no-longer-in-distress hobble away with her pack of mutts and looked down at my watch. If we didn't leave right now, we were going to be late.

I jumped out of my chair and walked over to Victor's side. "Come on, we can't be late for the meeting with Doussen and Associates."

Victor rubbed the back of his neck. "Should we offer her a ride? I feel bad for her walking on that ankle with so many dogs in this heat."

"We need to leave now or we're going to miss the meeting. You know how long it took us to get a meeting with a funding committee. God knows when we'll get another opportunity like this."

I started walking and heard Victor fall in step behind me. We hopped into my hand-me-down Lexus and set out for I-10. It didn't take long to get into standstill traffic.

"That was shitty of us to leave her," Victor said, staring out the window.

I could barely hear him over the air-conditioning and

the classic rock station blaring. That didn't stop me from turning up the music, just to be a dick. If he hadn't stopped to play hero, we could have left earlier.

When I noticed him looking at me with annoyance, I took off my sunglasses and rubbed them on my shirt. "What? She made it pretty clear that she didn't want our help. I don't know why you're still talking about her."

He shook his head. "Pay attention to the road, will you? What people say and what they mean can be two different things. I don't know how we're going to do in the meeting today if you can't grasp that subtlety."

"I was really planning on them being totally taken by your masculine charms. I thought that girl was going to swoon when she looked up at you and saw you looming over her. She was doing that eyelash batting thing women do in your presence."

"Nah, she was probably just blinking back tears from the way her ankle twisted."

If I hadn't been so totally preoccupied by my anxiety over being late, I would have laughed. As a rule, women got stupid at the sight of Victor; they found him that good-looking. It was too bad there weren't more women in venture capitalism—the Nacho-Copter would have been funded in five minutes.

"You gave her your business card, she'll call you to tell you she's all right, and you can invite her to dinner or something if you're that desperate to see her again."

"Jesus, Josh, you're heartless. Wouldn't you have wanted someone to help Esperanza if she found herself in a similar spot?"

My throat tightened at the mention of my sister. That was the problem with being best friends with your cousin —they knew exactly where your sore spots were hidden. I gripped the leather steering wheel and looked straight ahead. "Sure, but that's not exactly a problem with Esperanza anymore, is it?"

Victor's eyes softened and he looked out the window past the rows and rows of other cars all but parked on the interstate. "Sorry, man. I was just trying to make a point. But in general, wouldn't you rather live in a world where strangers help people in need?"

I swallowed and tried to crack a smile. "Rein in that hippy talk for the meeting or we'll never get the funding we need."

"You know there is one last option—"

"And it's out of the question."

"But it's what Uncle Kendall does—"

"Victor, for Christ's sake, stop bringing up my dad. We are not going to beg him for money."

"We don't have to ask him for money, just an introduction or two. We're not begging anybody. I wouldn't have quit my job if I didn't believe in the product."

We had to make it to this meeting on time. We had to make a good impression. We had both sacrificed too much. We had exhausted almost all of our options and all we had to show for it was a custom drone and a box of sales brochures. I'd be damned if I was going to ask my father for any more help.

Out of the corner of my eye, I saw Victor wave a hand. "Is anybody home?"

I cleared my throat as I watched the car in front of us inch two feet forward. A Toyota Yaris in the lane to our right tried to creep into the vacant space. I took my foot off the brake and rolled ahead. Then I settled back on the brake, aware of both Victor and the Yaris driver shaking their heads.

Victor cleared his throat. "Have you lost your voice, or did I do something to deserve the silent treatment?"

"Just thinking about the Nacho-Copter." I rolled my shoulders, trying to relax before the meeting.

Victor was quiet as we exited the highway and wound our way to the Santa Monica office of Doussen and Associates. We let the valet take the Lexus after we pulled out our files of promotional material and brochures, and finally, our prototype. Nervous as I was, the feeling of the drone in my hands made me giddy like a kid at Christmas. We took the elevator to the top floor of the chilly modernist building and exited to an office that was almost aggressively bright and angular. The art was blocky and the receptionist was all sharp edges too. I stood aside and let Victor work his magic.

"Victor Escalante and Josh Bowen here to see Mr. Doussen at three forty-five," Victor said to the receptionist with a smile.

The smile had the desired effect. The receptionist fluttered her eyelashes and blushed. "Uh, yes, hello Mr. Bowen, Mr. Escalante. Mr. Doussen's last meeting is running a little late. I don't know how you two managed to be on time with the traffic."

"Sheer force of will, I guess," I tried to joke, but the receptionist just looked at me like I had interrupted a private conversation between her and Victor. I shuffled my feet and looked at the door behind the receptionist's desk.

Victor recovered her attention without any trouble. "That's fine. Where would you like us to wait?"

The receptionist graced him with a glowing smile. "The waiting area over there has a television, a collection of magazines, and plenty of outlets for your electronic devices. Can I get you water, coffee, or tea?"

"Water sounds delightful."

The receptionist bounced out of her chair to grab a tiny bottle of water from a refrigerator behind her desk and presented it to Victor like it was the Holy Grail. She didn't so much as look at me, much less ask what I wanted to drink. I almost asked for a water of my own but I thought better of it. It wouldn't do to have the receptionist think I was an entitled son of a bitch. Which I was, but she didn't need to know that for sure until I secured her employer's funding.

We took our boxes and files and settled in the waiting area. Victor pushed the water bottle toward me.

"I'll get another one. I'm sure I could even ask her for a sugar-free mocha soy latte and she would happily run to a coffee shop to get it for me."

I snorted. Victor probably wasn't exaggerating, but I had never known him to abuse his power over women. I pulled out my cellphone and saw a text from my stepmother, Lana.

Hey Josh, I'm making baked ziti tonight. When are you coming home?

Tempting as it was to tell Lana that I had made other plans for the night, I knew my father would rake me over the coals for disappointing her. I didn't need this stress right now. I tapped out a curt response. *Hi Lana, I'm not sure, the meeting hasn't started yet. You guys can go ahead and eat without me.*

Lana's response was almost instantaneous. *That's ok, just text us when you guys leave the office and I'll start then.*

I couldn't argue with her, so I sighed and answered. *Thanks Lana.*

"What's up?" Victor asked, tearing his gaze away from the stock numbers breezing across the screen.

"Lana was asking about dinner."

The five minutes that followed felt like an eternity. I must have refreshed the email app on my phone enough times to set some sort of record. Miraculously enough, of the three emails that popped up, only one was a forwarded chain letter from Lana telling me and nine other people that she cared about us and hoped we would pass this letter on to ten more people. When the snooty receptionist finally announced that Doussen was ready to see us, I grabbed the drone's box and walked quickly into the conference room.

Doussen and several of his associates were seated around a U-shaped conference table. There were two chairs in front of the table, a television monitor, and a station for laptops to run presentations. Victor and I went around, shaking hands and giving out the information packets we'd convinced my father's assistant to print for us using the Bowen Corp copy card. As soon as the men on the other side of the conference table shook our hands, they started leafing through the packets and snorting. The lone woman in the room actually scoffed, "Nacho-Copter? This oughta be good…"

When everyone was settled, Victor turned to me to start the pitch.

"Good afternoon. Thank you so much for taking time to talk with us about our vision for the future of food services."

More than one eyebrow rose in response to that statement, but Victor nodded his head almost imperceptibly. I took a deep breath and continued, "We believe that for too long, pizza has had the prepared food delivery market cornered. Nobody makes it easier to order food than mainstream pizza chains. It's time for other restaurants to catch up, to perhaps leap ahead through the use of modern technology. Drones are here to stay—they might as well bring us lunch."

That got me a few laughs as I set up a short video to play about the Nacho-Copter. Victor had done a bang-up job shooting, editing, and producing the video. At the halfway point of our demonstration of the Nacho-Copter delivering carne asada breakfast tacos to a fire station, Doussen stood up.

"I think we've seen enough today, thank you. We certainly appreciate humor at this office, but we do not take kindly to our time being wasted. We welcome you to come back when you have a serious product that you would like to take to market. Good day, gentlemen."

Doussen marched out of the room with his head hunched over his cellphone and his goons trailed behind him. Victor threw his head in his hands and I sighed. That was it, a year of our lives, so much money and stress, for it to all fall apart. We'd known the risks going in, but we believed in the product so much, we thought we were different. We packed everything up and shuffled out of the room. The receptionist didn't acknowledge us as we left the office.

The valet brought our car around and we threw everything in the trunk. Once we were back on the highway to Brentwood, Victor asked, "So, what now?"

Chapter Three

ODIE

The crisp white front door to Granny's bungalow was wide open when I pulled up to her driveway. That was unusual. I parked the car in front of the house and listened carefully as I walked to the front door. There was nothing out of the ordinary, but I might have pounded on the door frame as I entered. "Granny! Granny! Are you home?"

When I heard no response, I shut the door behind me and started inspecting every element of my grandmother's home as if I was seeing everything for the first time. The calico quilt on the rose velveteen settee was covered in cat hair, and the dreamcatcher on the wall above the blocky television set had caught dust, if nothing else.

I shook my head. I needed to come by and help Granny with housework more often than I did. There was no sign of my grandmother in the front half of the house and I was beginning to get nervous. Right as I was beginning to wonder if I should call 911, I heard her reedy voice shrill some distance away. "Odie! I'm in the garden. I burned a pot when I was boiling water and I was letting the house air out. Come on back!"

I let out a breath I hadn't realized I was holding and trotted through the avocado green kitchen door into the backyard. The kitchen didn't smell like smoke...only when I embraced my tiny grandmother did I catch a whiff of burnt metal. I looked across the giant backyard where Granny grew the largest collection of lantana plants in Southern California, outside of Disneyland of course. Surrounded by tiny flowers that grew in bunches of every color imaginable, she was kneeling in front of a flower bed pulling weeds with her bare hands. The gloves I'd given her for Christmas were probably sitting in the shed filled with spider eggs. I didn't want to think how much dirt was crammed in the crescents beneath her nails. I just wasn't that fond of nature.

"Will you go grab my tin pail? I didn't think to grab it before I settled into pulling weeds, and now I don't think my knees will let me up and down anytime soon."

"Sure thing, Granny. Just promise me that you won't leave the front door open like that again. I nearly had a heart attack when I drove up to the house."

"You worry too much, Odie. I've been living on my own just fine for years and years."

"I know, but won't you humor your darling grand-daughter who's going to grab your weeding pail?"

"When you put it that way, what choice do I have?"

I walked to the dilapidated garden shed next to the house and grabbed the bucket Granny used to collect organic waste from her garden. She had a compost pile behind the shed, but she was picky about what made it into the pile—she liked to check everything before she added new material to compost. To help her cut down on that sort of work, I was seriously looking into getting a composting toilet for her birthday next month.

I was trying to imagine how she would react to a

present like that when she nudged me. "What'd you do to your ankle? You weren't limping yesterday."

I looked down at my ankle. I had forgotten all about it when I saw the open front door. I eased myself down onto the bench my grandfather had built for the garden and took off my shoe. The swelling wasn't pretty, but the pain was manageable.

"It's a long story."

"I bet it's not. I don't suppose you met any men for your troubles, did you?"

I thought back to Mr. Universe and giggled. Granny turned to look at me with sparkling green eyes. "Odessa Jane Ferguson, I never thought I'd be so proud of you. Do you have a date for Saturday?"

"Oh…well, he gave me his card, but that was because he was worried about me getting home safely. There wasn't any romance involved—none at all."

And I was okay with that. He was good-looking, sure, but I had it pretty good on my own. I had my dream job, all the sweet doggies I could ask for, good friends, and an appreciation for the wine country. There really wasn't anything more that I needed.

"It's just as well. Do you remember Lana Bowen from my Bible study? She has a stepson who's free for dinner on Saturday. I told her you'd be ready for pick-up here at seven."

"GRANNY!"

It was one thing for her to encourage me to go out on dates, but flat out arranging dates was just infuriating. I jumped up from the bench and felt my ankle twinge as I knelt down to Granny's level. Her eyes were dancing now, and the set of her jaw made it clear that she was ready and spoiling for a fight.

I locked eyes with her and huffed, "Mary Agatha

Parsons, where do you get off setting me up on dates without even asking me first?"

"When have you ever said no to a date I arranged for you?"

That question took me off guard. "Wha...?"

"Every time I call you to ask about a potential date, you go along. I didn't see the point of wasting cellphone minutes."

Damn my people-pleasing nature. I hated going on all of Granny's blind dates. She would arrange them for most of my Saturday nights and they never ended soon enough for my liking. But I just wanted to make her happy. After my parents died, she raised me, even when she really didn't have to, and I plain hated disappointing her. It took me a few minutes, but I finally found the words. "I don't like to be caught off guard. It feels like I don't have a choice. Can you see why I'm leery of that sort of thing?"

"I suppose, but it'll be good for you. I'm not getting any younger and I just hate the thought of leaving you on your own."

"Your physicals always come back perfect; I don't know why you're talking about leaving me alone."

"The long and the short of it is that I'm no spring chicken. I won't be around forever, and I want to see you happily settled before you toss me out on an ice floe."

"I would never toss you out on an ice floe! Shove maybe, but never toss."

Granny started laughing and before long I was laughing with her. Her huge calico cat came to investigate the commotion and started sniffing my muddy sneakers distrustfully. I stayed statue-still waiting for the vile beast to leave me be. When I stopped laughing Granny paused, but only started laughing harder when she saw my lip curled in disdain.

"Oh, thanks, Granny, laugh at my pain."

She came forward on her knees to pet her stupid cat. At the touch of my grandmother's bony hand on her head, the cat started purring like a Ferrari engine. Granny looked up at me with her white eyebrows up in her hairline. "See, she's a sweet kitty cat. Zsa Zsa has never hurt you, so I don't know why you're carrying on like she's a raptor from Jurassic Park."

"She has sharp claws," I said as Zsa Zsa kneaded the grass beneath her feet. Shredded blades of grass were getting caught in my shoelaces and my dogs were going to have a field day when I came home.

"Honey, you started a dog rescue. Last I checked, dogs can have pretty sharp claws too."

"It's not the same."

"Oh, sure. So what do you want for dinner? I have stuff for lo mein in the fridge."

"I really hadn't thought about dinner yet. But I need to go home and let the dogs out, they're probably ready to explode by now. Is there anything I can help you with before I leave?"

"You can promise you'll be here at seven on Saturday for that date with Lana's stepson."

I jumped to my feet and Zsa Zsa took off to hide behind a yellow-flowered lantana plant by the kitchen window. Granny stayed kneeling next to the bench, and I could have shaken her for wearing such a beatific look on her wrinkled, suntanned face.

"No." People-pleasing nature be damned; I was not going to let myself turn into a doormat!

Granny came to her feet, albeit more slowly than I did. At her full height, she just barely came to my shoulders. She somehow managed to look down her nose at me as she asked, "And why not?"

"I want a weekend for myself without any dates, without any employee outings, just Odie and her dogs, lying around drinking a bottle of wine."

"That paints a pretty sad picture, don't you think?"

"Granny, I'm happy with my life. I love my job, I love my house, I love my dogs and my friends. I don't need any of the complications a man brings. I've watched too many friends cry over men who've done them wrong. Excuse me if I just don't think they're worth it."

"Go on this date on Saturday and I won't set anything up for a month."

I looked down at my grandmother and shook my head. "No, and don't try any of your *Getting to Yes* tricks on me. This isn't something we're negotiating."

"I think you'll really like him. Just go on one measly date and I'll leave you alone for a whole month. That's at least four Saturday nights for you to get stupid drunk on wine with only your dogs for company."

"Your deal isn't more tempting when you put it that way. My time is mine and I can say no."

"But you won't. You hate to disappoint me after all," Granny said archly as she picked dirt from beneath her fingernails.

My shoulders pinched and I slapped a hand to my forehead. "Then it's kind of disappointing that you would try to use that fact to manipulate me. Here I was thinking you loved me, Granny."

"I'm manipulative, huh? Maybe my hearing is finally failing me, but I think you just tried to throw my love for you in my face."

Before I could stop myself, I had my arms wrapped around her narrow shoulders. "Oh, Granny, I was just frustrated, that's all. I'll go on the stupid date. But please, leave my personal life alone after that. I don't like fighting about this kind of thing."

She hugged me back. "Thank you, Odie, you've made my day. Now are you sure you won't stay for dinner? I don't want you overdoing it on that ankle."

"I won't, I just have to let my poor dogs out. I'll see you tomorrow."

As I squeezed her one more time, I saw Zsa Zsa take a running leap and pull a bird right out of the air. She picked it up in her mouth and dropped it at my grandmother's feet. I looked down at the pitiful twitching bird, then I shrugged out of Granny's embrace and tromped back to the house. Over my shoulder I called, "Oh, yes, what a sweet kitty cat. Tell that to the bird at your feet."

I closed the back door before Granny could respond. I really did need to go before the presents started piling up on my carpet at home.

Chapter 4

JOSH

I walked into my father's house and was greeted by the scent of expensive perfume and olive oil.

There wasn't any time to brace myself before a hand squeezed my shoulder. I looked down and saw my step-mother smiling up at me. "Hi Josh! Are you hungry? I bet you are after that was a big presentation. How'd it go?"

My shoulders tightened, but I tried not to look too downcast as I shrugged. "Hi Lana. It didn't go quite the way I had hoped."

Her lined face drooped and she patted my hand. "Awww, that's too bad. You'll just have to get out there tomorrow. After all, tomorrow is another day. In the mean-while, you can eat some baked ziti."

"Sure, that sounds great." I sighed and tried to smile.

"Dinner will be ready in an hour. Your father's holed up in his study." She paused for a moment, her forehead wrinkling. "He must be hyper-focused on something; he didn't even want to try the sauce."

"Good to know. I guess I'll be in the living room, unless you need any help."

"Oh, that's sweet of you, honey. Go along, I know my way around the kitchen."

That was only partly true. She knew how to boil water for pasta. My father's chef watched anyone who tried to cook in her kitchen with a scowl and no shame about jumping in when she saw imminent disaster.

I wandered into the living room and flinched at the sight of a new portrait above the fireplace. The picture was tinted in black and white and blown up to ludicrous size. Esperanza was in an oversized chair, smiling with her cat, Ceviche, in her lap. I remembered when Lana took that picture. Esperanza was in the middle of chemo. Her hair was totally gone and she was pretty tired and nauseous most of the time, but that day she was feeling well enough to sit up and play with Ceviche.

I stood there for a while thinking about the events that followed the picture, then I felt something brush against my leg. The fat orange fuzzball from the picture meowed up at me, hitting me with his tail. I stooped down to scratch his ears and saw my father round the corner of the hallway.

He paused and grimaced at the portrait. "That was Lana's idea. She's really proud of it. I hope you'll compliment her on it at dinner tonight."

I nodded, knowing better than to question his instructions even though he was looking at the portrait with narrowed eyes and a wrinkled forehead. If I didn't know better, I would say that he shared my distaste.

He didn't let the moment linger. "You had the meeting with Doussen and Associates today, correct?"

The tension in my shoulders returned. "That's right."

"Didn't get the answer you were hoping for?"

"No, not exactly."

"That's too bad. But it's normal. Don't give up." He paused. "I need to ask you a favor—"

My phone beeped and I pulled it out of my pocket to silence it. Victor's name flashed across the screen. *Quit feeling sorry for yourself and call me back, I have an idea.*

I snorted and killed the ringer volume before looking back to my father. "Sorry about that, Victor wants me to call him back. What was that you were saying?"

"When you call him back, tell him to come to dinner. Lana always makes enough food to feed the entire population of Los Angeles. But as I was saying, I need a favor. When Lana makes a request of you this evening, I don't want any fuss. You will agree with enthusiasm. Am I understood?"

I started to argue but stopped myself. My father was staring me down, all but daring me to contradict him. I could just imagine the guilt trip he had mapped out if I refused. But I knew how things were. He and Lana had let me move in when I was taking care of Esperanza, and hadn't said anything about moving out even though Esperanza had been gone for over a year now.

"Yes...can you tell me what she's going to ask?"

"I gave you a set of instructions, I expect you to follow them."

"I know your expectations, sir." I added that last bit for good measure. "But I don't see the harm in telling me what she's going to ask in advance."

"You may go change for dinner."

I went upstairs to my room, dialing Victor's number on my phone as I walked. He answered on the second ring. "Josh. Hey, where are you now?"

"My dad's house. Lana's making dinner. You texted while I was talking with him. Now he wants you to come for dinner."

"K, I'll be over in like twenty minutes."

"Weren't you going to tell me about your idea?"

"Two words: Professor Mun."

"What?"

"I'll be there in twenty minutes, I'll tell you more then."

The line went dead and I tossed my phone on the bed. A moment later Ceviche popped up onto the bed and started kneading the comforter. I scratched his head idly until I had an idea. He let out a comically un-intimidating growl when I got up and headed downstairs to the kitchen.

Lana was standing next to the stove with a glass of wine while my dad's chef stood by the sink shaking her head.

"Lana, Dad invited Victor to dinner tonight. I thought I'd let you know." I leaned against the wall between the kitchen and the hallway.

"Ah, I love that kid. Thanks for telling me. Maybe we should crack open a nicer bottle of wine than the two-buck chuck your father picked up on the way home from work."

"That's nice, but I don't think it's necessary. I know Victor's drunk much cheaper swill than that. He wouldn't want you to go to any trouble."

That made her laugh. "You two are such good boys. Did your father tell you about my little scheme?"

"He said you were going to ask me something at dinner tonight. He wouldn't say what, though."

"And I bet the suspense is just killing you. Doesn't it just drive you nuts when he wants to be cryptic and all?"

I pressed my lips together, not sure if agreeing, honestly or not, was the best course of action. "He likes to surprise people."

"You really are one good kid. So I'll tell you what, if

you promise to act surprised at dinner, I'll go ahead and tell you now. Deal?"

She stuck out a hand and I gave it a quick shake, which made her laugh. "Well then, one of the ladies in my Bible study has a granddaughter…"

Oh no…so this was why my father wouldn't tell me what it was. Lana kept talking, and I nodded and shrugged when it seemed appropriate. I was going to hear the whole thing over again anyway. I was more interested in figuring out a plausible excuse to avoid going on a blind date.

"…so what do you think?" Lana clapped her hands together and looked at me expectantly.

I hesitated, trying to mask the fact that I had stopped paying attention shortly after she started talking. "Um, I guess one date won't kill me."

She let out a really loud snort at that and I couldn't help smiling. How did such a good-natured woman end up with someone like my father? We both paused when we heard the doorbell ring. Moments later, Victor strolled into the kitchen with a bouquet of flowers. He held the flowers out to Lana and she wrapped him in a big hug.

"You are too sweet; you didn't have to bring me flowers! But these are lovely. I'm going to go find a vase for them."

After Lana wandered off, the chef let out a sigh and went over to the stove where she inspected the baking pan inside. I was about to ask if she thought it would be edible when Victor clapped me on the back.

"So what was this about Professor Mun?" I asked, turning to give him my full attention.

"He's helped past students get funding for their startups. The Nacho-Copter should be right up his alley. I sent him an email asking him to meet with us and hear our pitch."

"That's excellent. Let me know if there's anything I can do."

Victor studied me for a minute. "You don't sound that excited. It's the best thing I can think to do right now—"

"No, that's not it. I just had a weird conversation with my dad."

Lana came back into the kitchen, and Victor and I retreated to my room. I went into my closet to change for dinner, going out of my way to pick out my wrinkliest suit and my most obnoxious novelty tie. Victor sat at my desk and petted Ceviche until the cat swatted him away.

While I changed, Victor said, "So what did your dad say that made you so…pinched-looking?"

"Pinched-looking?"

"Yeah, you had this weird look on your face when you were talking to Lana, and I guess your conversation with your dad had something to do with that. What's up?"

"He issued a vague order without explaining himself. I talked to Lana about it and I think they're trying to set me up with one of her friend's granddaughters."

"Ah. It's just one date, though, right?"

"That's what it sounds like. I'll hear the details again at dinner when we put on a show for my father."

"Ahh. I'll try to be a good audience."

The bell rang for dinner and Victor followed me out of the room. Ceviche darted ahead of us. He was going to be waiting by Lana's seat to beg for scraps, no matter how much my father complained about it. The thought of my sister's dopey cat thwarting my father's will made me smile as I stepped into the dining room.

Chapter 5

ODIE

My date arrived on Granny's doorstep at seven o'clock sharp on Saturday night with a slightly crumpled bouquet of flowers. From where I sat, he looked all right: lots of dark hair, slim build, nice glasses, and full lips. Back in my tech startup days, he definitely would have been my type.

Granny met him at the door. "You must be Lana Bowen's stepson! You're every bit as handsome as she said. And you brought flowers—isn't that sweet? Please, come in."

Per Granny's instructions, I was waiting in the parlor on the rose velveteen settee, but I was considering making a break for the garden. The turquoise shift dress I wore made me feel fat, but Granny was certain that it made me look like Tippi Hedren at her prime. Because I didn't care about the date, I'd let Granny pick out the clothes and the hair. At best, the look had vintage charm, but I saw the way dear Mr. Joshua Bowen's lips twisted into a grimace upon meeting me.

He shoved the bouquet of wildflowers into my hands and said, "Do you need a minute to find a vase?"

It was like he was asking for an opportunity to run away. I closed my eyes and made a show of inhaling the faint fragrance before handing the flowers to my grandmother. "That's okay, Granny can manage. Shall we head out?"

Granny gave me a grin and a thumbs up from the window as I walked with my miserable date to his oldish Lexus. He went to the driver's seat and I was on my own opening the passenger door. The stupid clothes were even changing my expectations for male behavior! I sighed before opening the car door myself and buckled in. The sound of the buckle clicking was the last sound for a while once he started driving.

It was uncomfortable. I didn't want to be some weirdo staring at him or trying to make conversation only to be rejected by silence, so I just slid my eyes over to him every so often, then began to take my phone out of my clutch before deciding that that would be too rude.

When we came to the intersection of Babbitt and Graves, I finally said something. "Watch out for the stop sign, the tree branches hide it."

His knuckles tightened on the steering wheel and he managed to clip out, "I see it."

That was when I caved and pulled out my phone. I needed to scan the headlines for something—anything—to talk about this evening. I couldn't just stare at him for an hour or more in hostile silence. It wasn't going to play out like that; I was going to make an effort. News was pretty slow today—the headline was something to do with drones. I clicked through the article and started reading before I snorted.

"Why on earth would anyone want to own a drone?" I said almost to myself as I scrolled.

Out of the corner of my eye, I saw Josh's eyes widen as he turned to look at me. "Are you serious?"

"What's the appeal?"

He pulled into the parking lot of a fairly casual restaurant chain and hopped out of the car. He walked toward the entrance and I followed after him, wondering if, instead of looking through the news, I should have texted Crystal to ask her to call me earlier in the date than we'd planned. We went to the hostess stand and followed a waif-like blond to a table close to a giant bar. When she left us with menus, I looked across the table at him, deciding to needle him just a little. Anything to make this date seem to move along faster.

"So?" I asked, not bothering to open my menu.

He didn't look at me. "So, what?"

"I asked what was the appeal of drones. You sounded surprised when I made that comment about them in the car."

"I'm trying to get a drone startup off the ground."

Rather than let him see me cringe or blush, I tried cracking a joke. "I'd make some joke about turning it on first, but I really don't know enough about drones to make the joke work."

He scoffed. "Don't strain yourself trying to be clever, by all means. So what do you do?"

I nearly choked on the water I had just drunk, but I composed myself. "I run a dog rescue."

"Oh, that must be...something."

I opened my menu and started scanning for the more expensive items, but then I thought better of it. He didn't strike me as the kind of man who would offer to pay for a date. So I dialed it back and settled on pork chops with seasonal vegetables even though I really wanted the chicken parmesan. If I'd already stuck my foot in my mouth with the subject of drones, I wasn't going to tempt fate with marinara sauce. I put the menu down as the waiter came by the table.

"Good evening, can I get you two something to drink?"

Josh inclined his head toward me and I hemmed and hawed. "Um, I would like a glass of the Beaujolais, please."

"Make it a bottle, thanks." Josh handed the wine list to the waiter and went back to studying the menu.

The waiter briefly made eye contact with me and rushed off. I didn't pick my menu back up; instead, I pulled out my phone and started texting Crystal.

"Please don't text your friend to call you with an emergency. We'll never hear the end of it from our relatives," Josh said without bothering to put the menu down.

"How—?"

"I can hear your nails tapping on the screen. Believe me, I'm not dying to be here, either, but my dad would rip me a new one if I upset Lana by ditching her blind date."

"But if I left, it wouldn't be your fault—you stayed and stuck it out. I would be the bad guy. That would kill my grandmother, but I don't think we got off on the right foot anyway."

"We ordered the wine, we might as well drink it. I don't think they'd let us take it to go."

I giggled at that. "Maybe one of your drones could take it for us."

That made him clam up and I wracked my brain for something totally innocuous.

"Can you believe the heatwave we've had this week?"

"Really, we're going to talk about the weather?"

I folded my hands on the table and leaned across. "Then pick a topic you find more interesting. You've hardly said anything on this whole date, and I'm sick of trying to carry the conversation."

He let out a low, smooth laugh that sounded oddly familiar, and said, "All right, so how did you come to run a dog rescue?"

"I started the Rescue because I saw more and more Chihuahuas being dumped in the animal shelter where I volunteered. No one was doing anything to help this breed-specific crisis, so I started a rescue to help Chihuahuas and other small dogs who become victims of their breeds' popularity…"

Once again, he proved incapable of carrying on a proper conversation. He was studying me with his eyebrows knit together, so I just pulled out my phone and ignored him. I was checking my email when he said, "Did you hurt your ankle earlier this week?"

I put my phone back in my purse and regarded him suspiciously. "Uh, yeah, nothing serious. Just a little twist."

There he went laughing again. "I knew I'd seen you somewhere. You were walking all those dogs on South Sepulveda on Tuesday, and you fell when one of them went after the sleeping golden retriever."

"You were there?" I asked, wracking my memory of that day.

"My cousin grabbed the little dog that got away from you. We were getting lunch before we went to a meeting."

"Mr. Universe is your cousin?" I asked incredulously before I could stop myself.

Josh's ears turned red and he nodded. "That's not his real title or anything, but I'm sure he'd be flattered."

Looking now, I could see some resemblance, but that didn't stop me from wishing Mr. Universe had been sent on the date instead. I wouldn't have had a snowball's chance in hell with him, but he had much better manners than his cousin. Still, I turned at least four shades redder than Josh's ears and changed the subject. "So how did the meeting go?"

He opened his mouth and then closed it. Finally, he said, "It could have gone better."

The waiter saved me from digging myself further into a hole by bringing the wine and taking our dinner orders. When he left, I tried again to steer the conversation to safer territory.

"So what do you do for fun?"

He crossed his arms over his chest. "Why are you trying so hard?"

"I beg your pardon?"

"This date is a disaster. We have to suffer through it for our respective relatives, but we don't need to do the whole talking thing anymore."

I stared at him for a minute. "No, I'm afraid I can't sit in silence for another hour while we finish our meal and you take me home. I didn't want to be set up, either, but I'm not going to be more miserable than I have to be."

"Then we're at an impasse because I'm in a similar position. The only difference is that I would be more miserable talking than in silence."

That was when I decided to really have fun with the jerk across from me. "The meeting went that badly, huh? Must be hard to drive a Lexus and have a charismatic cousin."

"If I give you his number, will you shut up?"

"No need, he gave me his card. He was kind enough to help me…now that I think about it, if you were there, why didn't you come with him to help me up?"

The redness in his ears had just started to fade, but it flared up again. "He had it covered. Besides, I don't like dogs. Especially not Chihuahuas."

I blinked. "Are you afraid of six-pound dogs?"

"They're just lousy pets."

I almost threw my napkin on the table. A rabid dog would have been a better companion right now than this jerk. But I forced a smile. "Well, then, what is a good pet?"

He hesitated before saying, "Cats. They're smart, independent, and clean."

I couldn't help myself, I started laughing like a maniac. "Oh, that's perfect. Problem solved. We can suffer through this date and tell our families that this never had a prayer from the start!"

He raised his head. "And what makes you say that? I only ask so that we have our stories straight."

"Oh, now you're almost polite. That's just great. But if you must know, I hate cats."

"What's wrong with cats?"

"Where do I begin?"

The waiter came with our food and we ate in silence for a few moments before Josh said, "How are dogs superior to cats exactly?"

I tried not to smile. It was nice not to have to carry the conversation. "Cats are moody, untrustworthy, and recreational killers. Dogs are loyal, smart, and eager to please."

"But you were walking Chihuahuas."

"What are you trying to say?"

"I'm saying that my stepmother had a Chihuahua when she first married my father, and that dog was the dumbest, most willful thing that would sit on anyone's lap if they had cheese."

"But that's just one dog, not all dogs are like that."

"Well, not all cats are recreational killers. Ceviche couldn't be bothered to chase a mouse, much less kill it."

"Ceviche?"

"My sister's—er, my cat."

He took a sip of his water and started choking. I stood up and began slapping his back. He shrugged my hand away after a minute and I sat back down. The silence was really awkward, but I was ready for the date to be over.

"Sorry," he said.

"Ehh, this isn't the worst date my grandmother's sent me on. At least I won't have to go on another for a month or so."

"How many has she sent you on?"

"More than I can count. I don't love being set up by my grandmother, but she's an ace at guilt trips."

"Ah, that's…too bad."

The awkward silence settled over the table again, and I picked at my dinner until the waiter came and asked if we wanted dessert. Josh looked at me and I tried to avoid making eye contact. Josh waved the waiter away and he hurried back with the check. I dug into my purse for my wallet and pulled out my credit card, but Josh shook his head.

"My treat."

I wouldn't have called the date a treat but I forced a smile. "Thank you."

He gave me a thin-lipped smile in return and we got up and walked back to his car.

"So how did you get roped into this date?" I asked, just sick of the silence.

"My stepmother went to Bible study, told my father she wanted me to go on a date with her friend's granddaughter, and my dad told me that I didn't have a choice."

"They don't expect us to do another one of these?"

He laughed. "Well, I think they'd be thrilled if we made this a regular thing, but I don't imagine they want us to force anything."

"Sure."

"Well, let me drop you back at your grandmother's. If you want to, you should give Victor a call—he'd be thrilled to hear from you."

"I might."

The drive home was silent as I tried to remember exactly what it was that made Josh's cousin so appealing in the first place. He was stupid hot, but I couldn't recall what made him so spectacularly drool-worthy. I studied Josh out of the corner of my eye to try to jog my memory, but the man driving the car was just a blast of cold air, whereas Victor was warm and charismatic. I had his card somewhere. If Josh said I should call him after the date, I just might.

We came to a halt in front of Granny's house and I opened the door. I could feel Josh's eyes on me as I slid out of the car and onto the grass in front of the sidewalk.

"Thanks for dinner."

"Anytime."

I closed the door and walked up the path to Granny's house, all the while wondering if he really meant that. Once I opened the door, I heard the SUV's engine come to life. I checked inside and saw Granny asleep in the parlor. I closed the door behind me and pulled the quilt off of the back of the settee. Once I had her covered with the quilt, I heard a scratch at the back door. I opened it up and found Zsa Zsa with a baby bunny rabbit in her mouth.

So of course I screamed. I heard a snap, crackle and pop, and Granny was by my side. "Odie! Odie! Did that young man try to do anything improper?"

I bent down over Zsa Zsa and pried the rabbit out of her mouth. The rabbit hopped away, staggering a little as it landed each hop, and Zsa Zsa ground out a hiss. I shook my head as the cat stalked off into the night. "No, Granny, there was no chance of him doing anything like that."

"Oh…oh…is he a…confirmed bachelor?"

"Who's to say? I only know that he wasn't the man for me."

"Oh, well, that's okay. We'll try again next week."

"Granny!"

Chapter 6

JOSH

I had planned on a lazy Sunday morning after my awkward blind date, but those plans went out the window when I got a call from Victor almost immediately after I woke up.

"What, man? I was out kinda late last night," I said, making a pot of coffee as I got Ceviche's breakfast ready.

Ceviche wound around my legs, meowing and staring up at me with wide green eyes. I dropped his dish on the ground and he went straight to work inhaling his kibble.

"Good morning to you too," Victor said. "I take it the date went well, then? Wait, I'm not interrupting anything, am I?"

I snorted, almost choking on my coffee. "No, but it's early and I'd really like to go back to bed if you don't have anything to talk about."

"That's just the thing, I do. We need to get to Sullivan Canyon Park by ten thirty. Can you pick me up?"

That was curious, but seeing as it was seven forty-five, we were cutting it a little close. "What's going on? I don't remember any drone group meetups happening at that time."

"Professor Mun got back to us. He doesn't have time to meet with us during the week, but he goes to the park on Sunday mornings to fly drones. He invited us to come fly our drones with him and maybe talk about the Nacho-Copter. This is our shot. Can you pick me up?"

I didn't argue. Victor was big time into carpooling and his apartment was on the way to the park. I drained my coffee mug and poured myself another to bring back to my room. "Fine, fine. What all should I bring with us?"

"If you want to bring the Nacho-Copter prototype and maybe one of your personal drones, I can get some of our marketing material to show him."

"Oh, are we going to try to do like a formal pitch? I don't really want to wear a suit to fly drones in a park."

"Right, nothing fancy, just nice casual. You know, no basketball shorts."

"I'm not twelve, Vic, I know basketball shorts have no business outside the gym."

"I'm just saying, this is our shot."

"I heard you the first time. Now I'm going to hang up and get ready. I'll be by your apartment in like an hour and a half."

"What do you need all that time for?"

"I've barely had one cup of coffee. I'm going to need to at least three more if I'm supposed to be anywhere close to presentation mode."

"Fine, fine, just don't be late."

"I won't!"

I clicked the end button on my phone and hustled upstairs. Once I was showered and dressed like something out of a summer barbecue advertisement, I loaded my personal drone and the Nacho-Copter prototype into the back of my car. The drive to Victor's was pretty quiet. I ran into a little bit of traffic around some churches, but I was parked in front of his building at the exact time I had told him. I shot him a text, and a moment later he bounded down the stairs.

Once he'd tossed his own drone in the trunk and slid into the passenger seat, he ran a hand through his hair and turned the air-conditioning up. "Thanks for the lift. Did you bring the prototype?"

"I did. How are we going to fly four drones with only three people?"

"We don't have to fly them all at once. It would probably be better if we didn't spring the Nacho-Copter on him right away. I told him the general concept and he was intrigued, but I don't want to overwhelm him. So how was your date last night?"

"Well, remember that chick with all the dogs you rescued last week?" I tried to ask casually.

He fiddled with his travel coffee mug. "Errr, I don't remember rescuing any dogs."

"The girl took a fall walking a bunch of dogs and you grabbed the leash of the one that was running away. Ring any bells?"

"Oh, her! She never called me when she got home. I hope she's okay, we really shouldn't have left her on her own."

"She's fine. I saw her yesterday at dinner."

If I hadn't been driving, I would have watched his face for any reaction, but his tone was sincerely happy. "Small world, right? So how'd the date actually go?"

"She doesn't see the point of drones."

He had the mug to his lips and almost spat coffee onto the dashboard laughing. "Did she say that before or after you told her what you did for a living?"

"She was trying to make conversation, I guess."

"Ah, so are you going to see her again?"

"No, I told her to give you a call."

"What the hell possessed you to do that?"

I didn't want to tell him about her Mr. Universe comment. I mean, he had to know by now that he was God's gift to women. I didn't need to spell it out for him. "She remembered you and I think you two hit it off much better than we did. It was really the best thing I could think to do under the circumstances."

Victor huffed at that. "Has anyone ever told you that you are a huge ass?"

"Esperanza, once or twice a day."

Victor smiled but then paused. "You did the right thing by her. Your dad was really proud. Lana too."

I felt my throat tighten. I had a hard time with the sentimental stuff—I was more comfortable with jokes and barbs. It was easier for me to laugh than cry where my sister was concerned. We sat in silence as we pulled into the parking lot at Sullivan Canyon. In the distance, we could see a few drones racing above the treetops, and I cheered up just at the thought of flying my own drone.

Victor ran around to the back and picked up the cases for the Nacho-Copter and his drone. I grabbed mine and we headed down the gravel path to the clearing, where we greeted the other regular drone pilots who came to the park. We had just made it to the center of the clearing in the otherwise tree-covered park when we came across a well-dressed man with what looked like a small fleet of quadcopter drones.

"Professor Mun?" Victor called out, shifting the drones in his arms to wave at the man.

The professor slid his massive remote control into a leather messenger bag and turned to face us. "Victor

Escalante, it's good to see you again. This must be your cousin, Joshua Bowen?"

We trotted over to his side and shook hands. Once the niceties were observed, we started flying our drones. Once ours were in the air, Victor got down to business.

"We'd love to show you the prototype of our food delivery drone."

"Oh?"

"Yeah, we have it right here. Josh, can you get it set up to go?"

I picked up the Nacho-Copter's case, set the drone on the ground, and turned on the remote. The machine flickered to life and I brought it to hover in front of Professor Mun and Victor.

Professor Mun walked around the drone, nodding, and Victor gave a description of the specifications.

"And you want to deliver food with this thing?"

"That's the idea."

"How much money do you think restaurants make? How are they supposed to afford a drone like this?"

"Well, we were thinking this might be viable first for chain restaurants where there are more stores to split the cost—"

"Victor, I've got to stop you there. The margins in the restaurant business just aren't sufficient for a huge capital investment like a fleet of drones. I would love to help you, but I just don't think this is viable right now."

As he started to walk away, I said, "What would it take to change your mind?"

He paused, not bothering to turn around. "An entirely different product with a different business model."

I looked at Victor and saw his face was markedly paler than normal, but we both shrugged as if the rejection was nothing.

Victor managed to say, "It was good to see you again."

That made the professor turn around and smile faintly at his former student. "Likewise, Victor. Take care of yourself. It was nice meeting you too, Mr. Bowen."

He walked off, his fleet of drones trailing behind him. I took a breath and decided to do some tricks with my drone to try to distract myself from the anger and disappointment that was clawing at me. I did a series of barrel rolls, pitching the drone as high into the sky as I could and then bringing it plummeting back to the earth, only to pull up at the last minute.

"Well, if the startup doesn't work you can always go on the professional drone racer circuit." Victor sighed.

I parked my drone and socked him on the shoulder. "I'm not giving up now. Doussen and Mun aren't the only games in town."

"Can we just talk to your dad?"

"Oh, I'd rather we didn't."

Chapter 7

ODIE

When my alarm rang on Monday morning, I tried to roll over and snuggle closer to Woz, my three-legged Chihuahua. But then I remembered I was supposed to go into work early to finally talk with Crystal. She'd been so cryptic last week, but we had never found time to talk. That didn't mean her words had left my mind. On the contrary, the longer we put off talking, the more mysterious and foreboding her request to talk became. It didn't help that puppy season had come early this year and everyone, including Shereen, was racing to keep up with all the demands on the Rescue. Because we never got a chance to talk, we decided to put something on the calendar for first thing on Monday morning.

I rushed the dogs outside to go to the bathroom while I scrambled to get ready for work. Once all the dogs were inside again, I was off, pretty certain that traffic was going to make me late. When I got there, I realized that it didn't really matter. Crystal was waiting for me in the office with a pair of chai tea lattes. I pulled my chair next to hers and gulped down my latte. She grimaced as she took a sip of hers, and I couldn't help but say, "What?"

She looked at me with huge eyes. "I'm sorry. I know I'm being kind of dramatic, but I just don't know where to begin."

I sat back in my chair and took another sip of my latte to try to relax my nerves. "Whatever you have to say, I won't be mad. You know we can't afford to keep a firing squad on hand here."

She laughed weakly at the joke. "Well, it's funny you mention the subject of money. I'm trying to get my act together for law school next year, and I want to have savings so I don't have to work a bunch of outside jobs like I did when I got my bachelor's. I know money's tight around here and it wouldn't be right for me to ask for a raise. So I need to let you know that I'm looking for another job."

There was a lump in my throat as I swallowed a mouthful of tea. "I understand completely. I wish we could give you the raise you deserve right now, but you're right, money's not as abundant as I'd like it to be. I'm going to try to find the money, but I want you to know that I support you one hundred percent. Anyway, just know that when the day comes for you to move on, we're going to miss you around here."

"I hope I'm not crossing any lines asking to keep my job while I look for something else."

"Not at all, just give me two weeks' notice so I can find someone to pick up the work. Or I could ask Shereen to put in a few extra hours. We'll work something out."

"Don't bother with Shereen. You'd be better off writing up a list of responsibilities and tasks for your next employee."

I didn't want to think about that. "You could always

stay on as a volunteer, if only in an advisory capacity. I know law school is going to be busy."

Crystal got up and walked around the table to give me a hug. "I'll never be too busy for my friends. So, now that the guilt and anticipation isn't making me sick, let's hear about your date."

I leaned back in my chair and groaned. "Oh, you really don't want to hear about it. It was just the worst."

"Worst dates are the most fun to talk about. Would you say this was the worst date your granny's ever set up?"

I had to think for a second there. I pulled a couple of biscotti out of Crystal's desk drawer and pushed one to her before tearing into the other one. She ripped the wrapper open with her teeth and dropped the biscuit in her latte to soak. Finally, I said, "Yes and no. I mean, there was that beach bum who smacked the waitress's ass in front of me. But this one was pretty miserable. I literally could not stop putting my foot in my mouth. Then when I tried to text you to give me an 'emergency' call, he asked me to stop on account that we'd never hear the end of it from our relatives."

"Yeah, that's weird."

"I could not say the right thing. He barely laughed at any of my jokes. It was like he was laughing more at me than anything I said."

Crystal stirred her biscotti in her drink, staring off thoughtfully into the distance. "Some men are intimidated by smart, funny women. He was probably threatened by the fact that you were making more jokes than him."

"That wasn't a hard bar to clear. He wasn't making any jokes at all."

Crystal stroked her chin. "Well, I guess some guys are just assholes. You could always check Craigslist. Shereen seems to really like Mr. Aries."

"I'm really just looking forward to a break from all the blind dates. I gotta figure a few things out if you're going to go…" I almost said, "find another job," but I didn't want to sound like I was disappointed or angry with her. I really was proud of her—happy for her, even—but I was saddened by the prospect of her leaving. "…on to law school."

"Let me know if you want to kick ideas around."

We had just gone back to our separate desks when the smell of strong perfume assaulted my nose. Shereen walked in the door in high heels and a very tight-fitting pencil skirt. She took off her oversized sunglasses and shook out her hair. She smiled at her reflection in the window before turning around to greet us. "Hey ladies. Happy Monday!"

Crystal snorted but I returned the smile. "Happy Monday, Shereen."

"Last week there was something you wanted me to do for Diego. I didn't see any notes on my desk on Friday, so…do you still need help?"

I swallowed a sigh and didn't dare look to see Crystal's reaction. "Yes, I was hoping we could start a social media campaign to find him a forever home. He's such a good old dog, he really shouldn't be there in the back sleeping alone."

"Right. So what do you want me to do?"

"Wasn't your degree in communications?"

"Yeah, but what you're asking me to do is social media —marketing, really."

"How about you do some research on how other people have gotten dogs like Diego adopted? Can you email me a list of three possible plans by the end of the day?"

"Could you email me those instructions?"

"I think we gave you a notepad when you started."

"Yeah, but I used the papers to blot my lipstick."

"Oh, I see. Well, you can go get another from the supply closet if you promise not to use them to blot your lipstick anymore."

Shereen flashed a big white smile. "I'll even stick a note to my computer screen to remind me."

She clicked down the hall to the supply closet and Crystal turned to me. "Oh my God. Could she be any more of an airhead? Didn't she list social media as one of her proficiencies on her résumé?"

"Crystal, be real. Do you think she made her résumé herself?"

"Whatever you did when you were hiring Shereen, you should probably do the opposite."

"Right."

I turned on my computer and checked my email to see if anything had come in from the adoption match sites. There was a couple interested in the silly little white dogs, but I was more excited to see an email from the Esperanza Bowen Charitable Foundation. Purse Dog Rescue was a finalist for their annual animal welfare organization grant.

"Crystal! We're finalists! Maybe we can find the money to keep you after all!" I blurted, too excited to think about managing my expectations, or hers.

She sat up. "That's amazing! So what's the next step?"

"Well…" I glanced at my computer. "I've been invited to attend a finalist luncheon with the Bowen family next week. It's at the Hotel Soleil. No plus-one, though…"

"That's all right, I'll hold down the fort and make sure that Shereen does something to get Diego's campaign off the ground if she hasn't already by then. You just be your charming self and come back with that grant money."

Shereen came back to the office cluster, set a brick of

sticky notes on her desk, and stood quietly with her head tilted toward the kennels. "This might sound kind of crazy, but I think I heard a cat meowing by the back door. I mean, it was hard to tell over all the barking, but I'm pretty sure it was a meow I heard."

I looked at Crystal and we both sprang out of our chairs. We walked to the back door and listened. Shereen was right; it really did sound like there was a meowing sound outside. We went around the front, because we didn't want to set off the fire alarm, and found a half-open ice chest filled with kittens and a mother cat. There was no note or anything, but the kittens were so tiny their eyes were closed, and their mother was bone thin and looked like she had been through the wringer.

"We need to get them to the vet. Crystal, call ahead and let Dr. Adebayo know we're coming with new patients. Shereen, can you hold down the fort while Crystal and I take the kittens?"

Shereen was staring at the mother in particular. "If it's okay, can I come with you to the vet instead? Please?"

I looked at Crystal. Her eyes were crinkled and her head was cocked like mine too. After a minute, I blinked. "Sure. Crystal, are you going to be okay on your own?"

Crystal laughed. "Yeah, go already. God knows what's the matter with momma cat over there."

Shereen followed me to my car and insisted on sitting in the back seat with the chest, which we opened all the way to let the air circulate. We weren't worried about them hopping out, but Shereen fretted. "I don't want them sliding around more than they have to."

"Sure."

The drive to the vet was pretty quiet, with the exception of the occasional squeals of the kittens. As I drove, I tried to think of a time before now when Shereen had been so grounded and invested in what was going on. When we were five minutes from the vet, my curiosity got the better of me. "I've never seen you react to any dog this way. Why work at a dog rescue if you're so passionate about cats?"

She didn't answer right away, and I was almost afraid that I had offended her somehow. "We've never had puppies come to us this young. These kittens are helpless. It upsets me that someone would just dump them. I don't even know how someone could do that."

We pulled into the vet's parking lot and Shereen hauled the crate full of cats on her own. She didn't struggle with her heels or pencil skirt. I saw cat hair floating through the air and catching on her sleeves, but she wasn't at all concerned with appearances. It was like I was working with a stranger.

It was a relief to see Dr. Adebayo waiting for us behind the receptionist's desk. Dr. Adebayo's eyebrows rose to her hairline at the sight of us. "Crystal called and said you were bringing kittens. I had to see Odie come with cats for myself."

Shereen didn't smile at the doctor's joke. "Can we get them into an exam room? I'm worried about the mother."

Dr. Adebayo looked at me askance. She'd never met Shereen before. I nodded and the vet opened the door to an exam room. "Certainly, come inside…"

"Please call me Shereen."

When we got into the exam room, I hung back and let Dr. Adebayo and Shereen coax the kittens out of the chest. A couple of kittens came out willingly, but one was determined to stay next to its mother. Finally, Dr. Adebayo took the mother cat and Shereen took the kitten. The mother cat didn't struggle when the kindly middle-aged woman lifted her out of the crate, and barely opened an eye when the vet started to examine her.

After a couple of minutes of tense silence, Dr. Adebayo paged one of her techs. "We're going to need fluids for everybody. Formula for the kittens too—I don't think they've been able to get milk from mom for a while now."

Shereen shuddered and I put a hand on her shoulder as I addressed Dr. Adebayo. "Thanks for seeing them so quickly. Do you think you can take care of them until they're all adoptable?"

"I'm going to get them patched up, but we can't accommodate six kittens and a grown cat. We're full up here. I can contact a few cat charities I know of—"

"Before you do that, can I call my uncle first?" Shereen asked abruptly.

Dr. Adebayo looked at me and I shrugged, so she said, "Uh, sure. The tech's coming with the supplies. Fair warning, the cell reception isn't good in here. It's better in front of the building."

Shereen nodded and left the examination room. The tech came in shortly after, and they got the mother hooked up to an IV. The tech showed me how to give the kittens a bottle, and the three of us stood around the examination table feeding the kittens. I looked down at the kitten tugging at the bottle in my hands and smiled. Granny would never believe that I was so close to a cat of any kind of my own free will. But Shereen was right. These cats were so young and helpless, I couldn't summon my usual distaste for animals of the feline variety.

After a couple of minutes Dr. Adebayo asked, "So what's her deal?"

"Who, Shereen?"

"Yeah. Usually Crystal comes with you. Is she okay?"

"She's fine. She's just at the office. Shereen really wanted to come. She found the kittens this morning."

"Oh, I guess she's a cat lady. How does she get along with the dogs?"

"She's never shown a fraction of the interest she's shown in these cats."

"I'd love to hear the story of a cat lady working at a dogs-only rescue."

The tech and I both giggled, and a minute after that Shereen came inside. She was smiling pretty widely. "I talked to my uncle. He wants to foster the momma cat and kittens."

Dr. Adebayo and I shared a quick, confused glance while the tech asked, "Has he ever fostered kittens before?"

"As a boy, he rescued a litter of kittens in Tehran. I think if we give him a list of what he needs to do and what he needs to have for them, he can have everybody back to full health quickly."

Dr. Adebayo nodded. "All right, if you want to call him back with the address of the office, we can probably have everybody ready for him to pick up before rush hour."

I smiled, but then I thought of something critical. "How do we want to handle payment for today? Because they're not dogs, it really wouldn't be right of me to charge it to Purse Dog's accounts. I can take care of it, it just might require a payment plan."

Shereen's eyes went wide. "I can do it, Odie. I'm the one who found the kittens. Give me the bill, Dr. Adebayo."

Dr. Adebayo waved a hand. "Don't worry about it. If your uncle can come and fill out some paperwork, we can waive the fees for today's visit."

I breathed a sigh of relief. I was already paying out of pocket for Shereen's date to come on the winery tour. If I had to cover the cats' vet bill too, I would have been on a ramen noodle diet for at least a month.

"Let me at least give a donation so that other cats in need can get assistance." Shereen pulled her wallet out of her purse.

"That's very kind of you. When you go up to the front desk, you can talk with the receptionist about giving a donation."

While we waited for Shereen's uncle, we watched the kittens snuggle up against their mother. The mother cat wasn't breathing so heavily, and with the animals out of immediate danger we were able to relax. Shereen tried to brush the cat hair off her clothes, but the wiry fur was already embedded in the fabric. She gave up after a couple of sweeps. "The dogs will have a field day when we get back to the office."

"Yeah, but I have to say, I feel like I've just seen a whole new side of you, Shereen."

She laughed. "Despite my best efforts, I am a little bit more than just a pretty face."

I elbowed her. "Don't say things like that. You need to give yourself at least a little bit more credit. But I want to run an idea by you."

"Yeah?"

"Crystal might be leaving. I need to come up with some money if we're even going to have a prayer of keeping her at the Rescue. I'm going to this grant lunch for the Esperanza Bowen Charitable Foundation next week, but it just occurred to me that there may be a conflict of interest."

Shereen's eyes got really big. "We've got to find a way to keep Crystal around! After you, no one knows the Rescue better. I'll start looking for more grants…after I get

Diego's campaign started. But what was the idea you wanted to run past me?"

"Well, it's not so much an idea but something that just occurred to me. On Saturday, I went on a date with a guy called Josh Bowen. Do you suppose he's related to the Esperanza Bowen Charitable Foundation people?"

"Google it."

"I don't want to do that, it just seems too stalker-y."

She whipped out her phone and tapped something on the screen. A second later, she showed me her phone. "Easy. See, that wasn't stalker-y at all."

Right there on the screen was a picture of Josh Bowen at last year's Esperanza Bowen Charitable Foundation Gala. I found myself swearing. "So what do I do? I mean, is it a conflict of interest? I didn't know him when I submitted the grant application and we're not like in a relationship. The date was an abject disaster."

"So don't say anything. I bet he won't be there anyway."

"You're probably right."

Chapter 8

JOSH

Three walls of Hotel Soleil's banquet hall were lined with tables covered by presentation boards, flyers, and business cards for what looked like every animal welfare group in California. The one remaining wall had a large silvery-white screen hanging from the ceiling and a podium in front of it. A picture of Esperanza and Ceviche dominated the screen, and I tugged at the tie around my neck. I walked through the cluster of circular tables in the center of the room, trying to stay out of the way of the non-profit masses. For its size, the 2011 Esperanza Bowen Charitable Foundation's Luncheon for Animal Welfare Organization Grant Finalists was a subdued affair, and I wondered for the fifth time that day why my father insisted that I attend. I didn't have any influence over who actually won the grant, so the people who were trying to schmooze me were wasting their time and mine.

The only upside was that Victor had been invited too, and it was really something to see women of all ages, even women with blue hair and canes, fawn over him. As usual, he handled it well and gained more admirers in the process. What was the word Odie had used to describe him…"charismatic"? That was one word for it.

"Josh?"

I turned around and almost stumbled backward into one of the tables set for lunch. I never thought I'd see her again. What would she be doing here, of all places?

She brushed her bangs out of the face that I still dreamt about at night. When I didn't say anything right away, her smile faltered slightly. "Josh? It's me, Naomi. Don't you recognize me?"

How could I forget the first woman to stomp all over my heart? College wasn't exactly yesterday, but there are certain pains that take a while to fade. I finally found my voice, and it was a little bit shakier than I would have liked. "You…haven't changed a bit. What brings you to the grant finalist luncheon?"

Naomi's smile brightened at the compliment. "My boss likes to scout out promising charities and help them sort out their strategy to have a bigger impact in their field. He sent me to see if there was anyone particularly deserving."

"That's great. Um…gee, how long has it been?"

I knew the answer, but I figured it would make me sound cooler if I pretended otherwise. I remembered being friends in college, and I remembered being horribly in love with her and getting the courage to confess my feelings, only to have her admit that she was actually attracted to Victor instead. We were all friends back then, and it was really awkward to have her split from the group when Victor made it clear that he wasn't interested in a woman who would lead his friend along to get a better shot at him. Little did he know, he killed my love life in college right there. Once women knew that they couldn't use me to get to him, they all gave me a really wide berth.

She wrapped a strand of long dark hair around her

fingers and stared down at the floor for a minute. "Oh, umm...six years, I think? So what have you been up to?"

"Victor and I founded a drone startup."

"Wow! I bet it's going to be a hit. I just got engaged." She twisted a ring on her left finger absently. The respectably sized diamond caught the light and sent rays of light into my eyes. I couldn't say if the pain was from the light in my eyes or the strange surge of disappointment.

Ever since we had parted ways, I had imagined running into Naomi in the future. In those daydreams, I was always ridiculously successful, wearing a nice suit and an even better watch. Usually those dreams would involve me running into her with a woman even better looking than her on my arm. Stupid as those daydreams were, I basically wanted to be able to show her what she was missing. It was damned unfair that she all but got that moment instead of me.

Then I saw a familiar head of blond hair heading in our direction. I had an insane stroke of inspiration and said, "Congratulations, I'm so very happy for you. As it so happens, I've started seeing someone too, and here she is now. Odie!"

Thankfully, she turned, but she had a somewhat quizzical look on her face. She wandered over without prompting and I steeled myself as I wrapped an arm around her waist and laid a quick but solid kiss on her lips. For some reason, it all felt really natural, but I knew that I couldn't linger so I spoke quickly. "Naomi, this is my girl-friend, Odie Ferguson. Odie, this is my friend from college, Naomi Klein."

Odie took a step back and I gave her a big smile, trying to telegraph that I was begging for her to play along first and ask questions later. I must have been oozing despera-tion, because she smiled and took Naomi's outstretched hand. "It's great to meet you. Are you here with a nonprofit?"

Naomi smiled and launched into an explanation of her purpose at the gala, and Odie smiled and nodded. After a couple of minutes, I noticed my father enter the room and start circulating. I dropped my arm from Odie's waist but it was too late—he had noticed us. He didn't come over, but I saw a frown flash across his face before putting on his usual schmoozing mask. He flagged his assistant over and they shared a brief conversation.

"Josh?" Odie tapped me on the arm.

I blinked. "I'm sorry, what was that?"

"Naomi just asked you where we met."

"Oh, we met through family."

"And the fact that Odie is the head of an animal welfare organization has nothing to do with her reasons for dating the brother of the late Esperanza Bowen?" Naomi asked pointedly.

Great, not only had Naomi stolen my dream by flaunting her success in my face, she had barely said hello before trying to poke holes in the front that I'd slapped together to try to make my life seem less pathetic than it was. It was a second before I noticed Odie's head bow, and that made my stomach turn with guilt. I felt obligated to try to defend her. Pretending to be my girlfriend wasn't her idea. "We only went on our first date like two weeks ago and the grant application process for the foundation started long before that. Will you two excuse me? I think I see my father trying to get my attention."

That wasn't a lie exactly—his secretary was all but whistling for me. Naomi and Odie nodded and I left them to heed the secretary's call.

She cut right to the chase. "What are you doing with

that woman? Do you realize that you're embarrassing your father and the foundation?"

I scratched my neck. "She's doing me a favor. I roped her into pretending to be my girlfriend to save face in front of an old college friend. I don't see how this is any of my father's business."

"That woman is a finalist for the animal welfare organization grant. The sight of you canoodling with her at the luncheon is going to call into question the integrity of the foundation and the grant-giving process. We need to tell her that she's been taken out of the running."

"We weren't canoodling. I had my arm around her waist for less than five minutes. Please don't penalize her organization for my actions. She didn't volunteer for this scheme. We'll stop with the show. Will that make my dad happy?"

"I can't promise you anything. He's really not impressed with your behavior at the moment. But I'll talk to him."

I walked off, careful to try to keep some distance between Odie and me. Naomi probably wasn't fooled by my attempt to try to play Odie off as my girlfriend. She probably thought I was more pathetic than when she first saw me. I watched my dad and his secretary talk. From a distance it was hard to say whether or not they were going to do as I asked. I considered going over there, but Victor distracted me.

He clapped me on the shoulder and asked in a low voice, "Did you see Naomi?"

I pushed my hair back from my face. "I did, we already talked. I might have done something stupid."

"Would it have anything to do with the furious look on that blond lady's face? She's the woman we ran into the other week with all the dogs, right?"

I looked around to see where Odie had gone and if indeed she looked upset. Sure enough, she was talking to my father's secretary. I made my way across the room as quickly as I could, only to see her storm out of the banquet hall. My father's secretary tried to stop me with an outstretched clipboard, but I brushed past it and caught up to Odie in the lobby.

I grabbed her hand and brought her to a stop. "Odie, I'm sorry. I tried to tell them that it was all a big misunderstanding. Let me try to make this right."

She jerked her hand away from me and glared. "I think you've already done enough for today. I don't even want to know why you dragged me into that nonsense with Naomi—"

"It was stupid, I…" I trailed off, not willing to tell her exactly how miserable it was to look at the woman who had turned me down standing on top of the world while feeling like I was at the bottom. "I know you probably don't care why I did it. I'll admit it was totally selfish, but I want to make things right. I mean, if you made it this far into the grant process, your organization is probably pretty worthy. I want to help."

"Too bad. I wouldn't let you clean the dogs' kennels."

She hitched her purse up on her shoulder and hustled out of the hotel. I watched her leave, and a second later was joined by Victor.

He put a hand on my shoulder. "This hasn't been your month now, has it?"

"Shut up."

Chapter 9

ODIE

It was damned depressing going into the office the next morning. Yesterday I had been so hopeful, so sure that maybe the money to keep Crystal around was practically waiting for me, and today I was going to have to break some really shitty news to my team. I brought a grocery store box of scones and a travel carafe of coffee to the office to try to soften the blow.

"What happened?" Shereen asked first, smiling until she registered the scowl on my face.

I was dreading telling them the news and dying to set the heavy carafe down. "I'll tell you in a minute. Come have some coffee."

She followed me back to the office and Crystal looked at me brightly before dropping her smile. "How did the luncheon go?"

I put the scones and the coffee out and grabbed plates, napkins, and cups from the kitchen before launching into the story of how Purse Dog Rescue got screwed over by my asshole blind date.

At the end of the story, Crystal and Shereen blinked before saying in unison, "He did *what?*"

I stomped back and forth across the office. "He's been nothing but trouble. I can't imagine why I even went over to him when he called my name."

It was that people-pleasing flaw of mine. I never expected it to land me in a hard place professionally, not like this. When I got home from work, I was going to find someone—counselor, shrink, or therapist, whoever it took —to do something about this mad quirk that was steadily ruining my life.

"It's totally normal," Crystal assured me. "You shouldn't blame yourself."

But I do. I thought that grant was going to get me what I needed to keep you around here. Now I'm back at square one and you probably have like six dozen job offers already. I didn't say any of that of course. I splashed some coffee into a cup and stirred in some sugar, not caring if some went flying out onto the desk.

"Maybe he didn't mean for that to happen. He probably panicked and called you over to get him away from that college friend of his," Shereen guessed.

"But all the same, I'm out what could have been a sixty grand grant, and what's happened to him? He's fine; he'll live another day to play with his stupid remote control helicopters." I took a big bite from the scone as if the force of the action would make me feel better.

"He came after you though, right? That means something. An asshole just would have let you storm out of there without putting up a fight." Shereen persisted in giving him the benefit of the doubt.

"He said he'd try to make it up to me. I told him I

didn't want him to do so much as muck out the dogs' kennels."

Shereen straightened up. "I totally understand where you're coming from, but I think there's an even better angle here."

"Oh?" I paused, still not entirely used to seeing the serious Shereen.

She wrapped a lock of hair around her finger, examining the edges. "Well, he owes you a favor. He might not be able to get you a big grant, but I mean, he is a Bowen. There must be money or connections somewhere that you can cash in on. I mean, think about it."

Crystal snorted. "I think you'd be better off trying to get that Naomi woman's contact information. Not that you need somebody to tell you how to revamp your strategy, but I think it might be a nice kick in the stomach for him."

I shrugged. That suggestion was emotionally satisfying, but Shereen was speaking a certain amount of sense. "What did you have in mind, Shereen?"

Crystal wrinkled her nose slightly, but Shereen tossed her head. "Well, I would test out a medium to small favor first. To hear you tell the story, he sounded really guilty, and I bet you could get a small favor right away. So now that I'm thinking about it, I have an idea for a small favor. Like, you've been really concerned about Diego for a little while. Maybe call him up and ask him if he knows someone who can foster Diego."

I nodded, but there was one thing that came to mind. "He's not a dog person. He said so on the date. He has a cat."

Shereen laughed. "That's not a deal breaker. To do this favor, he doesn't even have to like dogs, he just has to know someone who does that can foster a dog like Diego. I bet he knows at least a couple people like that. There's basically no downside—you get to see if he's serious about redeeming himself, and Diego gets out of that sad little kennel in the back and into somebody's home."

And that would take the social media blitz for Diego off your plate for the time being too, I thought. But beyond that, I couldn't think of any more objections. At the end of the day, what did I have to lose by asking anyway? There was just one problem—I didn't have Josh's number or any way to contact him. I started up a Google search. Shereen made it seem less creepy than it felt, but then I remembered Victor's card from the day Carmencita knocked me on my ass. I dug my fanny pack out of my desk drawer and pawed around until I found the now bent and wrinkled business card.

I waited until Crystal and Shereen were busy to call. I didn't really want an audience, so I slipped into the back room with the kennels. I dialed and waited about four rings for an answer. I was flexing the business card in my hand when I heard Mr. Universe's smooth, rich voice. "Hello?"

"Victor, hi, this is Odie Ferguson, you saved my Chihuahua a couple of weeks ago…" I trailed off, not entirely sure how to get to the reason for my call.

"Yes, I remember, Carmencita! How's she doing?"

I heard a thwacking sound against metal. I looked over and saw Carmencita wagging her tail by the gate of her kennel. "Good, we've been working on her leash skills. She's still available for adoption if you're interested…"

He laughed. "Oh, I hope she gets adopted soon. So how's your ankle? Did you get it checked out?"

"It just needed some ice. Now I have a strange sort of favor to ask of you. Is now a good time to talk?"

"You got my attention, go on."

"I don't know if you heard, but I went on a blind date

with your cousin Josh a couple weeks ago. I actually need his number. Could I ask you for it?"

There was a significant pause on the end of the line. "Um...sure. Let me text you his contact information. Hang tight."

"Thanks."

I looked down at the card in my hand and found that I had creased it in half. A moment later, my phone buzzed and Victor was speaking again. "I sent it a minute ago, did you get it?"

I opened up my text message app and saw a phone number and name. "Yep, thank you."

"Anytime."

I ended the call and tapped the new phone number on my screen before I could talk myself out of Shereen's idea. It rang and it rang, and I was pretty sure I had reached the voicemail when I heard, "Joshua Bowen."

"Hi Josh, this is Odie from the other day. Um, I have a strange sort of favor to ask you if you can give me a call back—"

I was interrupted by laughter. "You didn't hit voice-mail, but I have to wonder, how did you get my number?"

"I called Victor—he gave me his card when my Chihuahuas helped me fall on my ankle, remember? Anyway, I don't want to take up too much of your time, but I need a favor."

"Go ahead."

"I need a foster for one of the Chihuahuas."

I heard him make an oohing sound. "I don't know—"

"I'm not asking you to take him personally, just to see if there's anyone you know who can take him. He's just miserable here alone. He's a big people dog."

"I can try. Is this your preferred phone number?"

"Yes. So Diego's housebroken and very laid back. I

wouldn't recommend him for a house with young children, but he'd be a great companion for an older person."

"I'm making a note of that right now. Let me ask around."

"Thank you."

We hung up and I went back to the office, where I found Crystal and Shereen had abandoned all pretense of working. Crystal had a particularly guilty look on her face, but Shereen had a look of unapologetic satisfaction. I put my hands on my hips and sighed. "So what'd you hear?"

"After the story you told, I was expecting to hear a lot more venom in your voice when you talked to Josh," Crystal said. "You did pretty well."

I shrugged. "I wanted to see if I could get that favor from him. He sounded like he was on board."

"Or maybe you were impressed by that kiss?" Shereen said, smiling like she was teasing.

I rolled my eyes. "Hardly. The man's been entirely too much trouble."

Chapter 10

JOSH

Victor called me to his apartment to talk about the Nacho-Copter, so I was surprised when I walked in the door and he greeted me by asking, "Did she call you?"

It took me a minute to figure out who he was talking about, but I thought I succeeded in sounding pretty casual about it. "Odie? Yeah, she asked me about finding someone to foster a dog."

Victor raised his eyebrows in surprise. "That's what she wanted to call you about? But you hate dogs. Are you going to do it?"

"I'm going to try. I feel bad about the grant thing."

"Who are you going to ask?"

"Lana, I guess. She probably knows some old fart who would like a temporary dog."

Victor shrugged and leaned up against the nearest wall in the living room. "Cool. But before you do that, you should probably go to your dad and ask for help with the Nacho-Copter."

"What? No!"

"Josh, we don't have any other options left. Professor

Mun was no help, Doussen laughed us out of the office, and we're getting toward the end of our rope."

I sighed. He was right, but I hated the thought of asking my father for help. "He's not going to make this easy. There are going to be strings attached."

"We're at the end of our rope, strings would be a welcome addition," Victor quipped.

I shook my head. "That was bad. But fine. I'll go home and talk to him."

"You do that. If that fails, I guess we can try crowd-funding."

"Wait, why aren't we trying that first?"

"Because like Professor Mun said, how many restaura-teurs have the money to throw at a project like this? We're not likely to get it funded as is. That's why we're asking your dad for help first. He can give us introductions, maybe to someone who could write a check and wait a couple years for the project to see some profit. Asking your dad for help would give us some more time to figure things out; crowdfunding would just give us a clock. Just talk to him, man."

"Fine, I'll let you know what he says."

I let myself out of the apartment and walked like six blocks to find where I had parked my car. Victor was right—we needed a break. He had his own apartment, but if we didn't figure something out he'd probably have to move in with his parents too. I owed it to him to try to spare him from that much humiliation. And it was humiliating to be a single man in his thirties living at home. Sure, in the wake of the recession, people tried to play it off as the new "normal," but even if the stigma was declining, it was still a decidedly suboptimal situation.

Once home, I made a beeline for my father's study.

After taking a second to straighten the cuffs of my shirt-sleeves, I knocked twice on the heavy door.

"Who is it?"

He always answered knocks at his study that way, even when it was just Lana and me in the house with him. I kept the exasperation out of my voice as I answered, "Josh."

"Come in."

I opened the door and saw my father tapping away at his laptop. Besides the frequent technology upgrades, the office had barely changed since I was a child. The inside of the office was all dark wood paneling, red Persian rugs, and leather-bound books on the built-in bookcases. It would have been impressive if my father hadn't told me that he had purchased the books by the yard when he first built the house. I stood there quietly, a habit he had drilled into me as a child who was prone to barging into the room to pester him. By now it didn't matter how long it took for my father to address me, I knew he would get to it when it suited him.

"It's been awhile since you've visited me during business hours. What brings you here? Don't tell me you got a Frisbee caught on the roof again?" He closed his laptop with a crooked smile. "Or maybe it's something to do with that woman from the luncheon?"

"No, she doesn't have anything to do with this. We really aren't involved. That was the girl Lana and her friend set me up with a few weeks ago. The luncheon was the first time we'd seen each other since the date." I didn't bother to mention that he was the one who'd ordered me to go on the date. If Victor wanted me to get his help with the Nacho-Copter, I really had to play nice. As hard as that could be sometimes with my father, I had to try.

"And yet…you were very comfortable putting on public displays of affection with her. It makes a father wonder…"

I shook my head. "All the same, that's not what I came here to talk about. I need a favor."

It hurt me to say that last part, it really did. I hated asking him for help. I knew he was going to lean forward and stare at me over his glasses in silence for at least ninety seconds while he tried to decide what was the best course of action for him.

Once the ninety seconds were up, he leaned back in his chair and steepled his fingers in front of his mouth. "Well, this is interesting. I've never known you to come to me as an adult for help unless you absolutely cannot avoid it."

"I wouldn't do it if it was just me who needed help—"

He chuckled at that and I could see the corners of his mouth curving upward. "Oh, this is interesting. Tell me, what do you mean, if it isn't just for you?"

"Victor and I talked, and he said at this stage of the startup, an introduction or two would be really helpful."

There, that didn't sound pathetic. That was almost dignified, even if the process of getting to the ask was anything but.

"I don't catch your meaning," he said, even though the twinkle in his eye made me think he knew exactly what I was after but wanted me to spell it out for him.

I had a hard time looking him in the eye. "Is there anything you could do to help us get the Nacho-Copter enough funding to go to the next level?"

He made me sit there in silence as I watched him weigh his options. He looked at me, he looked at his computer, he looked at the calendar hanging on the wall beside him, and finally said, "I suppose I can help you find someone who might be interested in a startup like yours. Now, I don't love doing this—it smacks of nepotism in my book—but I'm assuming you're asking for my help because

Victor needs things to start happening with the company. Is that the case?"

I nodded. "That's right."

When he gestured for me to sit in the chair across from his desk, I took a seat. It was rare that any of the conversations I had with my father in his office compelled him to order me to get remotely this comfortable. I was either in for a lecture or a negotiation.

Once I was eye level with him, he picked up a pen and a sheet of paper. Without looking up from what he started writing, he said, "I am willing to help with the Nacho-Copter, but I have one condition."

I knew there would be a catch, but I managed to keep my shoulders loose and relaxed. "Thank you for being open to helping us out. What's the condition?"

"You need to have a date for the Esperanza Bowen Charitable Foundation Gala. The board loves the story of your devotion to your sister as her health faded, but that story's a little old now. It just wouldn't look right if, a year and a half after your sister's death, you were living at home: without a steady job or significant friendships outside of your family. It would distract from the real purpose of the gala, and it would just look better if you had someone with you. And after that stunt at the luncheon, it would really be best if you could bring the same girl. I understand she might be inclined to say no, but it would still be best if you tried to convince her. If you show up with a new girl on your arm at every foundation event, it might give the board the wrong impression."

I swallowed and tried to choose the most diplomatic way to prepare him for disappointment. "That last part about bringing the woman from the luncheon might be a problem. I'm not sure she would want to attend another Esperanza Bowen Charitable Foundation event after she was disqualified from the animal welfare organization grant at the luncheon. I can ask her, but if she refuses would you accept a different date for the gala?"

"Do what you think is best. Just have a date in time."

"Okay, thank you. What should I tell Victor?"

"Let me make a couple of calls. I should have one or two potential leads for you by the end of the week."

"Thank you."

When he looked down at his laptop and put on a headset, I got up and left the office. I went down into the kitchen, where I ran into Lana picking at a bowl of almonds.

"Hey Josh!" she said brightly, only to tilt her head when she got a better look at me. "What's the matter?"

I forced myself to smile. "Nothing, everything's fine. But I have a question for you."

She pushed the bowl away from her and folded her hands in front of her on the table. "Oh yeah? Shoot."

"Remember Odie Ferguson?"

"That's Mary Agatha's granddaughter, right? Have you two seen each other again?"

There was a real edge of excitement in her voice, and I had to cut that off quickly. "Yeah, she was at the foundation's last luncheon. Anyway, she called me up asking a favor. Do you know anyone who would be open to fostering a dog?"

Lana's eyebrows arched. "That's a strange favor. She's looking for someone to foster a dog?"

"She has a small dog rescue, and there's an old Chihuahua that supposedly really needs to spend some time with people."

"Awww! I would love to have a dog around! Tell her we'll take him. This is going to be so much fun."

"I didn't mean for us to take him, I just told her that I'd ask you because I imagined you might know someone."

"And I do: me! I'll take care of him. You and your dad will hardly know he's here. Go call her and see what paperwork we need to fill out."

"All right. I'm sure she'll be pleased to hear we already have someone lined up. Thanks, Lana."

I walked up to my room and found Ceviche sitting on my navy blue duvet licking one of his armpits. He didn't acknowledge my entrance at all. If I didn't know the cat better, I would say that my father had set a disturbing precedent in the house. I scratched behind Ceviche's ears, then found Odie's number.

She answered breathlessly. "Purse Dog Rescue, this is Odie."

"Hi Odie, this is Josh. I found a foster for you."

"No kidding? That's great—fast too. I appreciate it. What are their details?"

"It's Lana Bowen, my stepmother. I think she goes to your grandmother's Bible study…"

"Oh, is she familiar with the work involved with fostering a dog?"

She sounded somewhat skeptical, and I had to take a second to think of something reassuring. "She had a dog when she married my father. She couldn't bear the thought of replacing him after he died, but she's really excited by the prospect of having another dog around. Would you like me to give you her number?"

"Yes, please, that would be great. Now, I don't know if I made this clear earlier but I don't allow just anyone to foster. I need to get an application filled out and sent back to me, and then I'll bring Diego by and see how he might settle in. Do you think she would be on board for that?"

"I imagine she would be. I'll be here to help in any event."

"Thanks, you really came through for me today. I might allow you to clean out my dogs' kennels yet."

I found myself laughing. "As you wish."

She giggled and took Lana's contact information. I hung up and found myself replaying the conversation in my head. "As you wish"? Where the hell had that come from?

Chapter 11

ODIE

Once I got over the weirdness of my last call with Josh—I mean, he was like the last person I would have expected to quote *The Princess Bride* at me—I got ahold of Lana to start the application process. She sent her application in the next day and it was clear that Lana was going to be a model dog foster. When I got her on the phone to go over her answers to the application, she was so solicitous and sincere that Crystal and I decided to expedite the foster evaluation process. We agreed on bringing Diego over to visit on the next Thursday.

When I told Granny the news, she insisted on coming with me and Diego to Lana's house. I told her it wasn't necessary. This wasn't a social call; I needed to be focused on how Diego reacted to Lana and her family. She told me to get over myself. I'm not sure exactly how she ended up in the passenger seat of my car with Diego in her lap, but she was all oohs and ahhs when we came to the Bowen Mansion. I'm sure that's not what they called it, but it would have put half of the houses in Beverly Hills to shame. It was set back from the road a ways and the landscaping was incredible. I nearly cried at the sight of the elaborate fountain in front of the house. This was what heaven on earth looked like.

"Who's that?" Granny asked when Victor came trotting out of the house.

He was just as gorgeous as I remembered. It was hard to think that such a warm, charismatic guy like him was related to a cold fish like Josh, but it was Josh's family that was taking in a dog, not him. "That's Victor. He's Josh's cousin."

"Well, damn. I'm sorry I didn't set you up with him."

I didn't really know what to say, so I hopped out of the car and ran around the side to grab Diego from Granny. She smirked at me when I took the dog like she knew I was at a loss for words. It had been hard to grow up with a human lie detector, and she was just as good now as she was when I was a rotten teenager. I set Diego on the ground and he sniffed the air around him.

When his tail began to wag, I smiled. "Soak it in bud, this could be your home in the near future."

He wagged his tail even harder, but paused when Victor came to stand in front of us.

"Is this Lana's new puppy dog?" he asked. "Wasn't he with you when Carmencita tried to take down that golden retriever?"

"Uh, yeah. He's not a terror, though, he's super chill." Right on cue, Diego flopped down to lie across my feet. "See?"

"Lana's on the phone but you can come on inside if you like."

"Yes, that'd be great. My grandmother insisted on tagging along—would it be a problem if she came inside too?"

"No, of course not." He walked around to my car and tapped on the passenger window.

Through the windshield, I could see Granny pat her hair and tilt her head to the side. I couldn't quite hear their conversation, but I could just imagine the compliments my grandmother was firing off at rapid speed. It might have just been the sun in my eyes, but from where I stood, it looked like Victor was almost blushing.

"Is this Diego?"

I turned around and saw Josh standing with his arms at his side. Immediately, I thought of that bizarre kiss and the way his full lips felt on mine, but I tried to push that thought from my mind. No, I wasn't going to think of that, I was going to focus on the dog. Still, seeing Victor and Josh together, I couldn't help but make a few comparisons. Next to Victor, Josh was paler, quieter, and less magnetic, but now seeing him for the third time, he had something Victor didn't. I couldn't quite put my finger on it.

When I noticed him studying me, I remembered that I actually needed to answer him. "Yeah, I think he's happy to be out of the Rescue."

Josh nodded and said, "It looks like Victor's keeping your grandmother entertained. Why don't we go inside and see what Lana's up to?"

"Yes, please, that would be great."

I followed him up a short set of stairs with Diego bringing up the rear. We stopped in the marble foyer and he slumped onto the cool tile floor. The sound of the collar and leash clanking against the floor was met with the sound of clicking heels. An older woman with pale blond hair piled up into a messy topknot on the crown of her head dropped to her knees in front of Diego.

"Oh, he is precious! He's like my last Chihuahua but fluffier! What's your name, cutie?"

She held out a hand for Diego to sniff, which he did for a moment before licking it. A second later he was in her arms, cuddling and kissing up a storm. Well, it was good to see that they were probably going to get along.

I held out a hand. "Odie Ferguson of Purse Dog Rescue—you must be Lana."

Lana nodded, barely looking up at me, her attention totally focused on the dog.

After a second of silence, I decided I might as well get on with Diego's introduction. "This is Diego. He's about eight years old and he has a little bit of a weight problem. As you can see he's very sweet, but I don't recommend leaving him alone with children. They tend to overwhelm little dogs like him. Did you read the foster information packet I emailed you the other day?"

"Yes, I did. I think we're going to have a great time together. I have a place for him set up in the mudroom. Why don't I get him settled in?"

She straightened up and grabbed his leash, then started to walk away, but I called, "I can come with you—"

"Oh, that won't be necessary, or if it is, I'll get Josh to bring you along. You should get him to give you and your granny a tour of the grounds. Kendall's really proud of his gardens; you should enjoy them." Her voice grew faint at the end as she rounded the corner with Diego at her heels.

Josh laughed softly. "They are nice gardens. Would you like to take a walk with me?"

I hesitated at the sight of his outstretched hand. "I'm not so sure. I haven't really enjoyed my last couple of encounters with you."

"Then, please, let's start over. Hi Odie, I'm Josh."

I snorted. "Let's not. But maybe we should see if Victor's taken Granny into the gardens. She gets a kick out of that sort of thing."

If I didn't know better, I would have said that he looked slightly disappointed. "All right then, follow me."

We walked back outside and around the side of the house to the most elaborate flower garden I'd ever seen. Well, there was more than just flowers—there were statues, benches, arches, and even more fountains yet. There was even a fat orange cat lounging in a copse of Russian olive trees.

"Ceviche! Get back inside!" Josh hissed.

"What, now?" I said, not sure I heard him right.

"That's my sister's cat. He knows he's not supposed to be in the garden. My dad would have a fit if he found him in here."

We went over to the cat and shooed him back toward the house, and he let out a low growl at the inconvenience.

"Now why would anybody want a nasty cat like him when they could have a sweet dog like Diego?" I said, genuinely curious.

"He has his moments. Besides, you never met Lana's old Chihuahua. That thing was a monster." Josh shuddered at the thought.

"If you say so. So where do you think Victor and Granny would be in all of this?"

"I'm not sure, but can I ask you a quick question?"

I should have known better than to say yes. Hadn't I said I was going to stop being a people-pleasing doormat? I almost said no, but I saw the way he was chewing on his lip. Instead, I heard myself say, "I…guess so?"

"Would you go to the Esperanza Bowen Charitable Foundation Gala with me?" he said in one rushed breath.

I had to take a minute to think if I'd heard him right. He didn't want to go on another date with me, not after the way he'd acted on the first date. Unless…no, it couldn't have been the kiss that changed his mind. It was silly of me even to think of it. So I said the most intelligent thing I could think of at that moment. "The what, now?"

He smiled faintly. "It's the big fundraising event for the Esperanza Bowen Charitable Foundation. I mean, you know the foundation's background after applying for the grant, I'm sure."

"Sure, but why are you asking me to go with you?"

I wasn't sure what answer I was hoping to get by asking that question, but I was at least entertained by the way he blushed at being put on the spot.

"Well, I don't have a date yet…" He trailed off but got visibly more enthusiastic when he had another thought. "And I thought that maybe you could turn it into a networking opportunity. There are people with a lot of money who're looking to donate—why not see who would be interested in an organization like Purse Dog Rescue?"

There was some sense in that. "But wouldn't that be bad form to go to one charity's event and try to get money and attention for my own charity?"

"It was bad form for my father's secretary to disqualify you from the animal welfare organization grant for just being seen with me. I don't think it would be terrible if you went to the gala as my date and maybe found a few potential dog foster parents or future board members."

"Well, when you put it that way, the invitation is rather tempting."

"But what's stopping you?"

"I don't know when the thing is, for one."

He grabbed his phone out of his pocket and tapped on the screen. A minute later, my phone vibrated in my purse. I had a good idea of what it was, and he nodded. "I just sent you the invitation. That should answer all of the logistical questions. Now, are there any other barriers preventing you from coming with me?"

I glanced down at my phone. I was free that Wednesday evening. As for his question, there was my conviction that men were nothing but complications. That was a pretty big barrier, but I wasn't going to say that. I shook my head. "I mean, you make a good point, but won't your dad be irritated to see me again?"

"To the contrary, he thinks it'll look better to bring the woman I was seen with at the luncheon than if I went alone."

"Is this another case of you being forced to go on a date against your will? If that's the case, I already know what's down that road and I'm going to have to pass."

There we go. That was assertive. I was totally not a doormat there.

He sighed. "Well, it's not a matter of being forced. It's a string he attached to a favor I needed. It was for a friend just as much as me, if that makes it any better."

"You have friends?" I couldn't help myself.

"Shocking. Well, I mean, it's Victor. Who could deny him help?"

He didn't know it, but that's when he got me. On the one hand, I was caving to my hatred for disappointing people and falling back into the habit of people-pleasing. But hey, it was a convenient way to explore whatever this attraction Josh held for me under the guise of helping Victor. It was really just a roundabout way of returning the help he gave me when I fell on the sidewalk. "Well, when you put it that way...what do I need to wear?"

He smiled and I was surprised to feel my knees go a little weak. He started talking but his words sort of washed over me because, to be honest, I was not only surprised but a little scared by the way he was making me feel today.

I heard Granny's laughter, and Josh paused. We turned to see Granny and Victor heading over to where we stood. Even from a good thirty yards away, I could see Granny's eyes twinkling, and I started to feel super awkward. One glance at Josh and the way he rubbed the back of his neck gave me the impression that he felt the same.

"Odie, can you believe these gardens? I hope Diego's not one for digging—can you imagine the landscape bill?" Granny laughed.

Shit, that was not a smart thing to say. What if they gave him back for fear that we had withheld information about his habits? "Diego's a very well-behaved dog, I'm sure the landscape's going to be just fine while he's around. Did you see Lana?"

"Yes, I did, I think it's love with that little dog. Wouldn't you agree, Victor?"

Victor was smiling, but I noticed that his admittedly gorgeous smile didn't have the same effect on me as Josh's. "I bet she'll have like seven different sweaters for him by the end of the week."

"Has the dog run into Ceviche yet?" Josh asked.

"Ceviche?" Granny asked with confusion.

"Josh's big fat orange cat," Victor explained. "No, we didn't see him on the first floor. That should be fun to see the two of them meet."

"Diego's very friendly, I'm sure they'll be fine," I said. "But if they don't get along, you can always give us a call and we'll come pick him up."

"I'm sure it won't come to that," Granny said. "Now I hate to cut this short, but we need to go if I'm going to make my chiropractor's appointment. It was lovely meeting you guys," she added at the end, batting her eyelashes at Victor but unable to keep a straight face.

Relief hit me like a ton of bricks. Good, it was time to

get out of there anyway, before I made a fool of myself in front of Josh. "Yes, we should head out before traffic really backs up. Thank you so much for taking Diego. Please call right away if you need anything at all."

Josh nodded. "Naturally."

Chapter 12

JOSH

As Odie walked out of the garden, my gaze drifted down to her rear. I realized I was staring a second too late, and Victor snorted. "Jesus, man. Her grandmother is literally right next to her!"

I punched his arm. "Could you say that any louder?"

We watched their blue Prius putter down the long driveway and then saw Lana walk out of the house with Diego on a lead. For such a little dog, he was doing a pretty good job of keeping pace, but his tongue hung out of his mouth the whole time. He might have been better behaved than Lana's last dog, but he still looked disgusting. And I was going to have to put up with this dog for at least a month, maybe more if Lana was really smitten with the thing. Ceviche and I needed our own place. But that wasn't going to happen until we got the Nacho-Copter funded. Speaking of which...

"I need to go talk to my dad. Hang around, we can talk about the Nacho-Copter after."

"Right. I guess I'll play fetch with Diego, then."

I jogged into the house and made my way into my father's office. We went through our usual performance for workday interruptions, but I didn't mind this time. I knew what I had to say and I felt pretty good about it.

Standing, I leaned on the back of the chair opposite my father. "I have a date for the gala now. Same woman from the luncheon too. So are we square now? Can you make an introduction?"

He looked over his glasses at me and gave me a close-lipped smile. "Good, very good. I have good news for you too. I already spoke to one of my acquaintances, Isaac Archambault. He has space on his calendar to meet with you and Victor sometime next month."

He pulled a piece of paper out of his desk drawer and scribbled something on it before offering it to me. "Call his office tomorrow and make an appointment. Don't wait too long or it will reflect poorly on me. I expect the meeting to go perfectly, am I understood?"

"Completely. Thank you for your help here."

He leaned back in his chair. "Don't thank me yet. So now that business is out of the way, what do you think of the dog?"

"I think he's already making Lana very happy."

"That's very good. Has he met Ceviche yet?"

"Not that I'm aware."

"It should be fine. If anything, it should be entertaining. Now, I have a call to be on with Stadt in five minutes, otherwise I'd come with you to see him. Can you see yourself out?"

"I think I can manage."

"None of that sarcasm at the meeting with Archambault, got it?" His tone was severe but the smile on his face was obvious.

I left the office and went back outside to find Lana and

Victor lounging on the patio, throwing a ball for Diego. He wasn't doing a very good job of fetching. He would amble over to the ball, pick it up and come flop down next to one of them to chew on it.

"Well?" Victor said when I sat down with them.

"He held up his end of the deal. We need to give Isaac Archambault a call tomorrow to set up a meeting."

Victor's jaw dropped and Lana grinned. "Oh, Isaac!" she said. "Tell him hi for me."

"You know Isaac Archambault?" Victor turned to Lana with a look of awe on his face.

"Know him? I was his executive assistant for ten years! He introduced me to Kendall."

I knew my father had met Lana through work, but I didn't know the details. "Huh, that's interesting. I don't suppose you could help us prepare for the meeting—?"

Lana turned to me and said in utmost seriousness, "Josh, I love you to pieces, kid, so I'm going to be honest with you. Isaac Archambault values honesty above all other traits in the people he chooses to do business with. If you go in there knowing his life story, or even with any information above and beyond what a person should have about his policies and preferences, he's going to shut you down. So as much as I'd love to help you out, I'm going to have to decline."

Victor nodded his head and I shrugged. "It was worth the ask. Thank you for telling us the truth."

We settled into a companionable silence. Then the housekeeper opened the kitchen door and Ceviche bounded outside at her heels. He sniffed the air and locked eyes with Diego. Diego wagged his tail slowly but didn't get up. For all his trouble, Ceviche rewarded him with a juicy hiss.

Lana laughed and petted Diego on the head. "He's just

not used to doggies; he'll learn you're a sweet boy soon enough."

My phone buzzed and I saw a text from Odie. *How's he settling in?*

I tapped out a reply. *He's made himself pretty comfortable. What's Purse Dog Rescue's position on dog clothing?*

Why do you ask?

Lana's already talking to the dog like it's a baby. Victor's probably right about the dog sweaters.

LOL! I'm glad they're getting along. Has he met your cat yet?

Ceviche saw him, he just hissed, the dog did fine though.

Good, let me know if you need anything.

Well, I didn't see that as a likely reality so I decided to try something out. *Do you want to do drinks sometime?*

There was a long pause, longer than it took for her to reply to the previous messages. *Sure. It's a busy couple of weeks for me but I think we can do drinks one night.*

I smiled. *Great, what about tomorrow?*

Ooooh…I'm doing an employee wine tour during the day. I can meet you after but I may not be in a drinking mood.

Coffee then?

That sounds wonderful. Do you want to meet tomorrow at 7?

I do. See you then.

"What has you grinning at your phone like an idiot?" Victor said, leaning over my shoulder.

I put the phone out of reach. "Nothing. Odie was just checking in on Diego."

"Awww!" Lana cooed. "Isn't she the sweetest? Mary Agatha did such a good job with that girl."

I started to ask what she meant by that, but decided it probably wouldn't get me anywhere given the way she had reacted to my question about Isaac Archambault. So I settled for a safe answer. "She's nice."

"Oh, please," Victor snorted. "Lana, you didn't see it, but trust me, those two are dancing around a really obvious attraction. You should have heard the things Mary Agatha said when we found them talking in the garden."

Lana turned to Victor with her jaw hanging open. "And where was I in all of this?"

"Getting Diego settled. Mary Agatha had a doctor's appointment so they had to go, but otherwise I'm sure we all could have sat around and watched these two try to ignore their obvious lust for each other."

"Victor, if it's not enough that you already look like a dark-haired Fabio, do you have to sound like you're narrating a cheesy romance novel too?" I ground out.

"See, it's obviously love. They don't know it yet, but I mean, when they're together, it's clear as day."

"Shut up."

That just made Lana giggle. "Are you bringing her with you to the gala?"

"Yes, I asked her to come with me in the garden. That's all we were talking about when Victor and Mary Agatha came out here."

"Oh, I'm so excited! You two are going to be the cutest couple there!" Lana clapped her hands together gleefully.

"You guys are going to have to do prom photos, it'll just be the cutest thing," Victor gushed alongside her.

That gave me an idea. "So tell us, Victor, are you bringing anyone to the gala?"

Lana froze and looked at Victor expectantly. He rolled his neck and sighed. "Nah, that's just not my style."

"Bullshit it's not!" Lana snapped, "I can talk to some of the ladies at the Bible study; one of them's bound to know a nice girl! Or Josh, you can ask Odie if she has any friends!" Lana was going at full steam and Victor started glaring at me. He was all but saying, "Look at what you've done."

I gave him a big shit-eating grin. "I'm sure I can ask."

"Don't bother." There was some real finality to his voice. I glanced at Lana. She had noticed it too.

"Oh, Victor, I'm sorry. We were just trying to help— playing, really. We didn't mean anything by it." Lana tried to soothe him. "But why? You're young, oozing with charisma, and you make just about every woman swoon at the sight of you. Why are you so against bringing a date?"

"I'm just not into LA women."

"Oh?" Lana leaned forward, very curious.

He rubbed his face with his hands for a minute before saying, "I'm looking for someone who's more direct and down to earth."

My reaction was almost automatic. "Good luck finding a woman like that in LA."

We both laughed at that one, but Lana shook her head. Diego jumped into her lap and started snoring right away. She smiled down at the dog. "I don't know, Odie strikes me as pretty direct and down to earth."

Victor looked anywhere but in my direction. "Yeah, too bad she's taken."

Is Victor jealous of me? It was hard to tell from the sound of his voice. I decided to play it cool. "I bet there are women who work at her rescue that might fit your criteria. But I won't ask her unless you want me to."

He gave me a small smile. "Get the Nacho-Copter off the ground and then maybe we'll talk."

"We have my dad's help. That has to be a step in the right direction."

Diego let out a huff and Lana smiled. "I think the dog agrees."

"And I think we're keeping the dog." I snorted.

Lana just shrugged. "Maybe."

I looked at Victor and we both shook our heads. It was obviously love.

Chapter 13

ODIE

Crystal had just settled into the passenger seat of my car for the third annual Purse Dog Rescue Employee Appreciation Winery Tour when Josh's name flashed across my phone's screen. I couldn't help but smile, and Crystal took full notice.

"He texted you? Ooh, somebody has a crush!" She giggled and made kissing sounds.

For a moment I was sad that Shereen and her boyfriend took his car—they could have saved me from Crystal's teasing. But it was just the two of us, and there was no one and nothing to deflect her attention. Carpooling suddenly seemed like a huge mistake. But we knew from past experience that some of the wineries had really small parking lots, so carpooling had become a practical and cost-effective team-building exercise. It didn't get much better than that for a nonprofit.

"He texted me good morning; it wasn't a marriage proposal. Calm down," I said, trying to play it cool.

"He was thinking about you, that's a critical starting point. And where there's smoke, there's fire. You texted back, right?" Crystal said, eyes twinkling as she buckled her seatbelt.

"Yeah, it seemed like the polite thing to do."

Crystal snorted and was quiet for a minute while I backed out of the Purse Dog Rescue parking lot. It was a nice day, a little overcast, but that was better for the winery. Traffic wasn't too bad as we wound our way out of town toward the vineyards to the north. When we were on the open road she started after me again. "So what'd you say?"

"I said good morning back and asked how he was doing. I wasn't sure if he had a question about Diego or anything."

"You dropped him off yesterday. Besides, Lana is Diego's foster, she would be the one texting you with questions. No, he's clearly interested in you. So was there anything more than 'good morning'?"

"He asked if we were still on for coffee tonight."

"What?" Crystal slapped the center armrest, her outrage clear in her tone. "You didn't tell me you were going on another date with him! You should have told him to come with us! It would have been fun."

I rolled my shoulders. It most certainly would not have been fun to have Crystal, Shereen, and Shereen's Craigslist date study my interactions with Josh. I said, "One, there's the issue of cost. I couldn't very well invite him to come on the tour and then ask him to pay his own way. That would be tacky. Two, I want to get some work done between the wine tour and coffee. I'm still trying to find the money to keep you around, you know."

Crystal winced. "Yeah, I know. Thank you, by the way. I know it's been a frustrating couple of weeks for you."

"It's not your fault. So how's the job search coming? Any good leads?" I asked, maybe too brightly.

"Can we talk about something else?" She shifted in her

seat, suddenly very interested in the scenery outside her window. "Maybe your texts with Josh?"

I conceded in an effort to make her feel more comfortable. The winery tour was going to be markedly less fun if Crystal was in low spirits. "Well, he thinks Lana's going to be one of those people who puts clothing on their dogs."

"Aww! But that's not what I meant. I mean, after the way the blind date and the luncheon went down, I'm stunned that you're giving him the time of day."

"He asked me to go to the Esperanza Bowen Charitable Foundation Gala with him."

"That's intense. How'd he con you into that?"

"He had a couple of good reasons. Some made sense for the Rescue. Supposedly, I might be able to scope out some donors and board members."

"I don't buy it. You might have used that reason to justify it to yourself, but deep down, you wanted to go with him. I don't blame you. I mean, he's the first guy to catch your attention in a while and some amount of self-delusion is normal. I'm just excited for you, is all I'm trying to say."

That was really sweet of her. "Aww, sweet as that is, you might try dating for yourself for a change."

"Nope, too busy trying to scratch the money together for law school, studying for the LSAT, and getting my application materials together. Dating can wait. I'll just live vicariously through you until I have time to try for myself."

"Oh, Crystal, but if not now, when?"

"When I'm a partner at an intellectual property law firm. Not a day before." Crystal looked off into the horizon as if she could just picture the future she described.

I snorted. "You get entirely too excited by even the prospect of a good morning text for me to believe that for a second."

"Shush. So where are you meeting Josh for coffee?"

"Uhhh…we never nailed that down. I'll text him later."

"Right, so what's the story with the gala?"

"Well, it's next Wednesday. I need to find a dress."

"You haven't gone dress shopping already?"

"I mean, I've been busy. There's been a lot going on with Granny and the shelter. It's also worth remembering that he only told me about it yesterday. When was I supposed to have time to shop?"

"Forget fundraising after the tour, let's go shopping instead."

"I really don't have the money for it right now."

There was a sharp silence that fell over the car like a scratchy wool blanket. Finally, Crystal said, "You used your own money to pay for Shereen's boy toy's part of the tour, didn't you?"

"It's fine. Shereen really surprised me with the way she handled the abandoned kittens the other day. I'm happy to do it."

"But it's not right."

"I'll go by a thrift shop and find something. It'll be fine."

"You can't go to an Esperanza Bowen Charitable Foundation Gala in some cast-off homecoming gown! That's insane!"

"I'll find something nice. I just need to give myself a chance to recover from the unexpected expense, that's all."

Crystal was shaking her head as we pulled up to the first winery on our itinerary. It was a beautiful piece of land with a gentle creek off to the side of the property and a bunch of flowering wisteria trees. The winery itself was enormous—two stories with pillars and tall barrels of wine lining the side of the building. A low-end luxury sedan pulled up next to us and Shereen bounced out of the passenger side.

"Hello! Ladies, I'm so excited to introduce you to my boyfriend, Bradley Westminster IV." She waved her hand as a tall man slid out of the driver's side door. He was immaculately dressed in a pair of crisp khaki chinos, a cool blue sport coat, and gleaming aviators.

"Please, call me Brad. It's a pleasure to meet you ladies. Shereen loves working at the Rescue. It was very kind of you to invite me. Shall we go in?"

There was an oddly robotic, almost bored, quality to the way he delivered his introduction. I shot a quizzical look at Crystal and she shrugged.

"Yes, I think the entrance is that way," I said with a tight smile.

He nodded and snapped his fingers. In an instant, Shereen was hanging on his arm and his hand was drifting past her waist. When their backs were turned, I looked at Crystal and she had the same wide-mouthed expression of horror on her face.

"Did he just...?" I asked, to make sure that I wasn't hallucinating.

"I think he did. What black lagoon did he crawl out of before Shereen found him on Craigslist?"

We shook our heads and followed Shereen and her horrific boyfriend up the cobblestone path to the entrance of the winery. We walked through the elegantly aged oak doors and were greeted by a woman dressed in a sleek black pantsuit.

"Welcome to Winery de los Patos," she said grandly.

That made Brad laugh. It was a really grating guffaw. "Winery of the duck? What kind of an establishment is this anyway?"

The woman gave him an icy smile. "It's a winery

founded next to a duck pond. Ducks featured frequently in the winery's history. We thank you for your feedback."

Brad turned to us and gave us a look at his perfectly even, blindingly white teeth. "Let's find someplace else. One of my buddies went to the Royal Flush Vineyards the other day and said it was top notch."

"We already booked a wine tasting here. Going to the Royal Flush Vineyards doesn't fit our itinerary," I ground out through gritted teeth.

Shereen looked back and forth between me and Brad anxiously. "I'm sure it's a fine winery, Brad, it just has an unusual name. Can we try it?"

Brad looked down at Shereen and stroked her hair. "Of course, baby doll, whatever you want."

The lady in black didn't do a very good job of concealing her disappointment as she walked to the hostess stand and pulled up our reservations on the computer. "Four for Ferguson? Right this way, please."

She led us down a long hallway lined with windows that revealed great silver fermentation vessels and other winemaking equipment. As we passed each one, she described what it did and how the winery managed that stage of the process. Brad yawned several times and the hostess didn't bother to hide her scowl by the third one. At the end of the hallway was a giant wine bar with an assortment of tall tables and short bistro sets.

The hostess addressed me, angling her body as if to exclude Brad from the conversation. "Would you like to sit at a table, or would you rather be at the bar?"

Crystal shivered and rubbed her hands up and down her arms. "Wherever is farthest away from the A/C vents, please."

Laughing at that, the hostess led us to a tall table near some windows overlooking a small green pond. "There isn't much sun today, but there should be enough to keep you from freezing."

I smiled at her. "Thank you, this will be perfect."

As the lady walked away, my phone dinged with a new text message. I waited until we were seated before I discreetly pulled my phone out of my purse to see who it was from. Granny was at tai chi today and then she was going to lunch with some of her girlfriends. Nothing should have come up. I wracked my brains to think who else might be texting me, but there was only one person that it could be. I could see the smile forming on Crystal's face. One glance confirmed that my suspicions were correct—it was Josh. And he was being a little bit flirty.

I feel silly. We've had two separate text conversations mentioning our date and we haven't specified a location in either one. Where would you like to meet tonight?

My breath came out in a whoosh. It must have been louder than I realized because Shereen tore her gaze away from Brad and asked, "What's the matter, Odie?"

Crystal elbowed me. "Go on, text him back. I'll bring her up to speed."

I snorted but didn't protest. To Josh's text I replied, *Hah. Yeah, that's on me too I guess. Umm…what about the Java Factory?*

Let's do it. Do you want to meet me there or do you need a ride after your wine tour?

Nah, I'll meet you there.

See you tonight.

Shereen grinned at me when I looked up from my phone. "So how's Josh?"

I shoved the phone into my purse, determined to focus on the winery tour going forward. "He's good."

"I bet he is. Crystal said he's taking you to the Esperanza Bowen Charitable Foundation Gala."

Before I could answer, Brad jumped into the conversation. "Nice. Kendall Bowen is the man. I like to think of him as a mentor, personally."

"How nice."

"I'm still waiting on my gala invitation; it must have been lost in the mail or something. I retweet Kendall's tweets all the time."

"Right."

A waiter came along and brought us a plate of chocolate disks and a bowl of oyster crackers. Shereen inched away from both, but I could see Crystal's fingers itching to dive into the crackers.

"The som will be along momentarily with a sample of our wines. Enjoy."

As the waiter walked away, Brad snorted. "How cute, he called the sommelier the som. This really is a classy joint."

I caught Shereen's eye and she wrinkled her nose just the slightest bit in acknowledgement. Crystal dug a handful of crackers out of the bowl and I took a handful of the chocolate. It was terribly childish, but I was tempted to throw some of the candy at Brad when his head was turned.

The som came by and introduced herself as Andrea. She pulled out her corkscrew just in time for Brad to snort, "That's nice, little girl, but will you get the real som?"

Andrea blinked a couple of times before she answered slowly, choosing every word with obvious care. "I am the sommelier at Winery de los Patos. What can I help you with today?"

Brad drummed his knuckles on the table. "This place is a joke. Women can't be sommeliers, everybody knows that. Let's go somewhere else."

I cleared my throat. "Andrea, I'm so sorry. Where can I

settle our bill? We'll come back without our caveman next time."

Brad guffawed. "Excuse me?"

Andrea gave me a hesitant smile. "I'll give the bill to the gentleman here. After all, it's impolite to let a lady pick up the tab."

She swept off and Brad pounded his fist on the table. "This place is a disaster! I will be leaving a review of my experience on all of the social media websites! Your days are numbered, Duck Winery!"

Shereen coughed. "Brad, I don't think this is going to work. Why don't you see yourself out now?"

"What do you mean, baby doll?" Brad was all gentle tones and soothing arm pats as he spoke to Shereen.

"I mean, you were rude to the hostess and the sommelier. That's a big red flag behavior."

"What are you talking about?"

"You were rude to the waitstaff. If you can't treat strangers with respect, what kind of treatment can I expect to receive? Anyway, I don't think we should see each other anymore."

Brad stood up abruptly, making his chair groan as it slid along the painted concrete floors. He nearly upset the table, and Crystal set a hand on either side to keep everything steady. "I know when I'm not wanted! I can't believe you would choose this dump and these ugly bitches over a date with me. Enjoy growing old and dying alone!"

He started to walk out of the tasting room, but Andrea caught up with him. She shoved a leather folder into his hands. "Sir, you almost forgot something."

He huffed and said, "I didn't eat or drink anything, I don't have to pay."

"You were served snacks. You can pay or you can go to the back and wash dishes. The choice is yours, sir."

"I'm calling my lawyer."

"Do, after you settle the bill. Security knows not to let you leave without paying."

He reached into the breast pocket of his sport coat and pulled out a leather wallet. The logos on the wallet were visible thirty feet away from the table where we sat. He slammed down a piece of plastic into the folder. Andrea gave him a bow of her head and walked over to the computer situated behind the bar. A moment later, she had a receipt and pen ready. Brad scribbled on the receipt and tried to pocket the pen.

"Sir, I believe you have our pen. Should we add another five dollars to the tab?"

"This isn't a five-dollar pen!" he fumed, but threw it over his shoulder as he walked down the hallway.

Once we heard the great oak doors slam, Andrea bent down to pick up the pen and set it down on the bar. She walked back over to us and smiled. "Well, that was fun."

Shereen was beet red. "Oh my God, I am so sorry. I had no idea he was an asshole. He was really sweet when we first met."

Crystal scoffed. "He snapped his fingers for you to take his arm as we walked into this place."

"He's just an alpha male," Shereen said weakly.

"I think the word you're looking for is alpha-hole," Andrea volunteered.

After we stopped laughing, Andrea clapped her hands. "So, now that the asshole's out of the way, let's have some fun. I'm thinking we should start with that Pinot Grigio, then go on to a special house red and finish with a port. Does that sound good to you, ladies?"

We all nodded and Andrea rubbed her hands together. "Excellent, I'll be right back. Please keep snacking on the oyster crackers and chocolate. The asshole paid enough for you guys to eat here for the next week."

Crystal laughed. "Don't encourage me, I'm tempted."

A few minutes later, Andrea came back with the wine and we were drinking and carrying on.

"So what are you thinking of wearing to the gala?" Crystal prodded.

"You don't have a dress already?" Shereen asked, eyes wide with shock.

"No, I haven't had time to go shopping."

"Well, the asshole paid for this winery, so you can probably afford to shop someplace nicer than a thrift store now," Crystal said, careful not to look at Shereen directly.

I didn't think Shereen's eyes could get any bigger but they almost bugged out of her head. "Oh, Odie, why did you let me bring him if it was going to cost more than you budgeted?"

"I didn't want to disappoint you—you were so excited about him."

"You're the boss, you're allowed to tell me no. I would have understood."

Shereen was just full of surprises. I never thought about my hatred of saying no and my position at work. I was the boss. Shereen could be ditzy but she wasn't unreasonable. Once again, I hadn't given her enough credit. I didn't like letting that moment stand, so I said, "Well, it's water under the bridge now. Let's do some team-building."

"Look at you, all businesslike on an employee winery appreciation tour. What's lit a fire under you? Would it have anything to do with those text messages you were sending earlier?" Shereen giggled.

"No. Well, it made me realize something. Shereen and I have been distracted by guys so far and that's not what this event is about. I should apologize—I know better than that. That said, it's been a year since we've gotten together to specifically appreciate each other's contributions to Purse Dog Rescue, and I'm so happy we're together here today. Now, I say we stop talking about guys and start talking about things we can do to keep our team intact."

Crystal cringed but Shereen sat up straighter.

I took a breath before continuing. "I want to make it clear that I support our team wherever their paths take them, but that said, I won't be happy with myself if I don't at least try to keep us together. So this is as good a way to team-build as any. Let's try to figure out what we can do to stay together. I know we're all really busy, so this is why now is the perfect time to put our heads together to think of new fundraising angles."

Crystal crossed and then uncrossed her legs and didn't say anything. Thankfully, Shereen slapped the table and blurted, "What about this place?"

"What about it?" I said, looking around to see if there was anything I'd missed.

"Why don't we ask them to sponsor us?"

Andrea came around just in time to hear Shereen's last question. "Sponsor what?"

Before Crystal or I could say anything, Shereen was off. "We run Purse Dog Rescue in Los Angeles. It's a rescue devoted to helping small dogs, and we're trying to figure out better ways to fundraise. Do you know if the winery sponsors charities?"

"Um…" Andrea paused. "You know, I'm not totally sure. Let me talk to the owner. Do you have a card?"

"I do," I said, and fished a card out of my purse.

Andrea looked it over and tucked it into her pocket. Then she told us about the house red she was pouring for us and left us to our conversation.

"I don't think she sounded too enthusiastic," Shereen said, swirling wine in her glass.

Crystal took a deep whiff of her glass. "I'm not sure I agree. But really, though, the worst thing they can say is no. Now, Odie, I'm going to bend the rules about talking about guys for a minute, okay?"

"Just try to keep it to a minute, please," I said, draining my glass.

"When you see Josh tonight, make sure that good old Brad isn't on the guest list."

I pulled out my phone to remind myself to do just that. "Good idea."

"And now back to our regularly scheduled programming," Crystal said. "So do you think Diego's foster might keep him?"

"I feel like you're trying to be sneaky here. But it seems like she's a big fan of Diego."

"I'm hurt by your lack of trust! That's good to hear. Shereen, how are the kittens doing?"

"Oh, they're good. My uncle loves having them around. So Odie, have you thought about the next favor you're going to ask Josh?"

"I really haven't given it that much thought," I said, but that was only half-true. I had thought about the gala and how much I was going to enjoy finding donors right under Kendall Bowen's nose.

Chapter 14

JOSH

I met Victor at his apartment to prepare for the meeting with Isaac Archambault. We had called his secretary as my father instructed and set up a meeting for the eighteenth of the month. Victor was bound and determined to make our pitch the best it could possibly be, and he wanted my help to create a newer, less corny demo video.

"Josh? Anybody home?"

Victor was waving a hand in front of my face. I smacked it away. "What?"

"You're not focusing. Your dad gave us this introduction, and if we embarrass him in front of Archambault we can forget about getting any more help."

"I know."

He went to the kitchen, then came back with a couple of Red Bulls and offered one to me. I refused. If I was going to get coffee with Odie later that evening, I didn't need the caffeine making me more anxious than I already was.

I mean, I liked this girl, so it was natural, normal even, to not want to screw things up. I shouldn't have a prayer with her. I'd already made a mess of things, so I didn't know what I was so afraid of. That first blind date was a disaster and the luncheon was pretty bad too. Things had picked up since Odie called me out of nowhere, but everything just felt so tenuous. But hell, my past interactions with her had probably set a low bar for her expectations. Somehow that wasn't very comforting.

"Do we need to get you some Adderall? What's it going to take to get you to focus?"

He had laid out a bunch of papers on the table and I hadn't even noticed. I lied anyway—he didn't need the aggravation of trying to put me back on track. "No, I'm paying attention. I just have been doing a lot of thinking."

"There's not time for thinking, we have to get ready for the meeting."

"I know; we will. I just have something else going on and I don't really know what to do."

He sighed and rubbed his forehead. "All right, if talking about whatever's on your mind will get you back on task, let's get going."

I didn't really want to talk about it. I expected more in the way of teasing from him than anything else, but he was right—we did need to buckle down and get things done for the meeting.

"I'm meeting Odie for coffee tonight. I'm just trying to figure out how I got here," I blurted out in one breath.

Victor's reaction was everything you would expect: a couple of confused blinks and then a cleared throat. "Are you…regretting asking her out?"

"No, I just know my pattern."

"Your what?"

I ran a hand through my hair. "My pattern, you know. We grew up together, you know how it goes with me."

He shook his head and I groaned. "Forget it, it's stupid anyway."

We sat in silence for about a minute before Victor's eyes widened. "Is this about Naomi? Are you still hung up on her?"

"No, not anymore! I mean, it was particularly bad with her, but she was just one in a long series of women who…" I trailed off, realizing that what I was about to say was going to make me sound like a whiny little bitch.

"Women who…used you? Naomi was crazy; what she did was pretty fucked up, but not all women—"

"Just all women who've laid eyes on you have wanted you more than me."

"But she's not going to the gala with me."

I let out a hissing breath. "She only agreed to go because I told her it would help you."

"I'm sure that's not true. But I can try to keep my distance at the gala if that would put your mind at ease."

"No, if she's after you, she's after you. I'll just try to be happy that I have a date that my dad approved of."

"Ugh, dude! If she was so into me, she wouldn't have agreed to coffee with you. You need to stop selling yourself so short."

"That's not true. This wouldn't be the first time I asked a woman on a date only to have it turn into a sly fact-finding mission centered around you. Maybe I should cancel it."

I went to pull out my phone and Victor socked me in the arm. "This. This is the kind of attitude that's keeping you unhappy. If you cancel now, you're going to (a) feel terrible and (b) have a super awkward time at the gala. You don't want either of those things—I know you."

"Fine. Fine. I'll go, but if you come up in conversation

more than three times tonight, I'm just going to check out."

"That's your decision. You're being ridiculous, but I think we've done enough talking for the moment. Can we focus now?"

"Sure, sure, fine. What were we talking about?"

He sighed and said, "You know what, let's forget the marketing material for now. Let's go fly the drone for some new demo footage. That'll be fun, right?"

I hopped out of my chair. "Sure. I just have to leave in time to get to the coffee shop by seven."

"You got it."

We packed up the drone and Victor grabbed his video camera. We went to the nearest park and got everything set up. Every so often a curious walker would come by and ask us questions, and we took it as an opportunity to gauge reactions to the Nacho-Copter.

"That's crazy. My uncle owns a restaurant—he could never be bothered with that technology!" one middle-aged woman scoffed before power walking down the trail.

I shrugged when Victor looked crestfallen. "Maybe we should have stayed in and worked on our pitch."

"No, it's fine. The weather's perfect for a video. Let's just get this over with. You'll probably need to shower before your date."

I rolled my shoulders and winced at the way my shirt stuck my back. Grimacing, I said, "Yeah, I think you're right."

We took the drone through a couple of simple exercises and fielded a few more questions. Finally, someone came along who saw the merits of the technology.

"Yeah, I mean, why does a person have to sit in a car, in traffic, with only a bag of takeout as their passenger?" he said. "That's the perfect starting place for drones. Cars would come off the road, people would find other work, and who knows, our food might even arrive faster. I think it's great."

Victor smiled. "Would you mind letting us quote you in our marketing material?"

"For a fee, maybe?"

I grimaced. "If we had funding, we would, but we can't really do that just at this moment."

"Oh, well. Have a nice day, gentlemen."

The guy walked off and Victor shook his head. "I would have given him the five dollars in my wallet."

"But that would be like paying for a review. If Isaac's as ethics-conscious as Lana says, that might not impress him."

"Right. Never mind that, then. So we have the footage we need; are you ready to head back?"

"Sure."

I volunteered to drive so Victor could start looking through the footage on his computer and decide what we needed to do next. Then we parted ways and I raced home to shower and get ready for the date. No one was home, and that was just as well because I would have felt terribly self-conscious trying on at least four different shirts before settling on one, leaving the rest crumpled together on the floor. Ceviche came into the room and promptly settled on top of the clothes.

"Wish me luck, buddy."

Ceviche started licking his butt, and I took that as a sign of all the support I was likely to get. I petted him anyway and headed back out, this time to the Java Factory. Despite the traffic, I got there early.

I sat in my car and checked my phone. There was no text from Odie so I had to decide: go inside and wait for her as the only person in the coffee shop alone, or stay in my car and wait until I saw her. But that last option would probably come off kinda creepy. I fiddled with the cuffs of my sleeves for a minute before stepping out of the car. If I was going to be the lone weirdo in the coffee shop, I was going to take a minute to polish my appearance.

Then a familiar blue Prius rolled into the parking space next to me, and Odie was out a moment later.

"Well, how's that for perfect timing?" she said as she came to stand next to me.

I caught a faint whiff of alcohol on her breath and said, "Hi Odie. Did you have fun on your wine tour?"

"Yeah, once we ran off Shereen's awful date, we had a pretty good time. By the way, could you check the guest list for the gala?"

"Probably, why?"

"We just need to make sure that Bradley Westminster IV isn't on the list. To hear him talk, he seems to think of your dad as some kind of mentor."

I let out a snort. My father was never one to mentor. "Not likely—Brad dated Esperanza briefly. He was way more into conversations with my dad than with her. Lana wouldn't let him within ten miles of the funeral."

Odie smiled at the mention of my stepmother. "How is she doing with Diego?"

"Good, I think he's settling in pretty well. Ceviche has stolen his food a couple of times, but he didn't get bent out of shape over it."

"Is he at least getting something to eat?"

"I probably shouldn't tell you about Lana's bad habit of slipping animals scraps from the table, should I?"

Odie just snorted softly and shook her head. "Normally, no, but at least I'm not worrying about poor old Diego starving."

We walked inside and ordered coffees before sitting

down. There was an awkward silence and I cast around for something to say.

"Are you ready for the gala?"

She bowed her head. "I haven't really had a chance to do any shopping..."

I shrugged. "That's understandable. I mean, you only got the invitation yesterday. Can I help you with anything?"

"You really don't have to."

"You're coming as my guest—I didn't mean to inconvenience you. Are you sure I can't set something up for you?"

When Odie hesitated, I waved a hand. "You don't have to decide right now. Just call me if you want any help. So you had fun at the winery? I'd love to hear more about that."

She launched into a description of her coworker's date, and I made a point to nod and cringe in the appropriate places, but more than anything I had a great time watching her talk. She didn't talk with just her face and mouth, but used her whole body. At one point she almost tipped the table over.

"Whoa, are you all right?" I said, catching her coffee mug before it could topple off the edge.

She sighed and wiped at the table with a napkin. "Fine. I just got a little excited. But I will admit that I'm getting kind of tired. I hate to cut this short but I think I need to hit the sack."

As soon as the words left her mouth, I couldn't help but imagine what it would be like to go to bed with her. The coffee shop suddenly became at least ten degrees warmer, and I definitely noticed her eyes widen as she turned more than a little red.

"I'm sorry I wasn't more entertaining company," she said as she rushed to gather her bag and get up.

"No, not at all. Have a good evening, and do give me a call if you decide you want help finding a dress."

To my great surprise, she leaned across the table and planted a soft kiss on my lips. "You taste just as sweet as you sound."

She swept out of the room on that note, and I sat there in shock for a good five minutes before one of the baristas announced the coffee shop was closing. She was just tipsy, but I shouldn't have let her drive. And I shouldn't have let her kiss keep me up that night, but I tossed and turned anyway. What had I gotten myself into?

Chapter 15

ODIE

I was feeding the dogs breakfast when my phone started ringing. What was someone doing calling at eight on a Wednesday? I suspected that it was probably Crystal or Shereen asking why I was running so late. Well, I'd stayed up until two in the morning dress shopping online and had a hell of time waking up. I was pretty sure that I'd nearly squashed Woz when I rolled out of bed. I still needed a dress. The gala was tonight and I didn't have a dress or anything else I needed to look even remotely sophisticated. Correction, I had a nice neutral evening bag. But that was about it.

There was too much to do today. I mean, if the phone was already ringing, clearly I was needed at work, and I just didn't have time to go freaking shopping.

The phone rang again and I realized that I still probably needed to answer it. So I dropped the dogs' bowls on the floor and raced back to my bedside table. "Hello?"

"Odie? Is this a bad time?" Josh's voice was clear on the other end of the line.

"Oh, no, no, I just had to engage in some athleticism to get to my phone. What's up?"

He laughed. "Um, Diego is acting a little strangely. He was dragging his backside along the grass this morning."

"Oh, that? Well, that's actually pretty normal for dogs of his age and size. You're lucky he's doing it outside and not on your carpet. I mean, we can take him by the vet to get it taken care of, but it's really a pretty minor thing. Is Lana bothered by it?"

"No, she wasn't fazed at all. I just saw him doing it and thought it was weird."

"Oh, well, ring me if you need anything else. But while I have you on the phone…does your offer to help me find a dress for the gala still stand?" I added that last part kind of sheepishly.

There was a short pause on the other end of the line. "Uh, yeah. We can definitely get you kitted out. Do you have any free time today?"

I let out a hissing breath. "Well, I mean, it's busy at the Rescue, but I can move things around. I'm sorry I'm just now asking you for help—"

"It's all right. Can I put you on hold for a few minutes?"

"Oh, sure."

"Thanks."

The line went silent and I rolled out of bed. I made a beeline for the coffee maker in the kitchen and let the dogs out the back door. The coffee maker had just finished filling my cup when I heard Josh say, "Odie, are you still there?"

"Yes."

"I just got ahold of a family friend. She has room in her schedule today to style you for the gala. Can you be there at ten?"

I winced and took a sip of my coffee. "I—I mean, I'm thankful that you got your friend involved, but I...Well, what's her fee?"

That was embarrassing to say out loud and I wasn't surprised by silence on his end of the line, but my pride was stinging. If I was struggling to find a dress online in my price range, what were the odds I could afford a stylist and whatever dress and accessories she piled on me?

"I'm sorry it wasn't clear earlier, but I want you to know that this is my treat," he said slowly, with a lightness I wasn't used to hearing from him.

I couldn't have asked for a more generous offer, but it didn't soothe my pride at all. "Oh, that's very kind of you but I can't accept—"

"Please, you're doing this for me as a favor. I'd feel guilty if I accidentally gave you an undue burden and you didn't give me a chance to make things right."

"It's not that, really. You really helped me out with Diego."

"But I was the one who put you out of the running for the grant after kissing you in front of everybody. You probably could have slapped me and saved yourself a lot of trouble."

"Ehh, but what's a kiss between friends?" I found myself saying, and in that moment I was very glad we were talking on the phone because I was a horrible shade of red.

He laughed at that. "Exactly, so what's a dress? Nothing—less than nothing. Anyway, I already asked Xandra; she's excited to help. Just have fun, okay?"

"I..." I trailed off, casting about for objections. "It's peak puppy season and the Rescue has been so busy. And then there's Granny, she's been wanting help with some of the shrubs in her front lawn..."

"I can ask Lana to send Dad's landscapers to help your

granny. The dress shopping probably won't be an all-day thing—you can probably head back to work for a couple hours afterward. Let me send you the details and you can sort out some time away from work."

"Fine." I mean, I was a little excited by the prospect of ducking out of Granny's gardening task, I just didn't want him to have the satisfaction of hearing me agree with any more enthusiasm.

"I'm glad you're letting me help you. I know you're not one to ask for help, so it means a lot that you asked me."

"Don't read too much into it," I teased.

He laughed. "I'm going to send you the information now. Call me if you have any questions or need anything else for the gala."

"Thank you."

"No, Odie, thank you."

We hung up and my phone buzzed a second later. I took one look at the address and texted him back immediately. *Are you sure I need a dress from a place on Rodeo Drive? Can't I just go to a department store?*

He texted back right away. *You'd be surprised by the kinds of deals you can get on Rodeo Drive with the right connections. Just remember to ask for Xandra. Also, bring a bag for extra clothes.*

I'm not okay with this. You will pay.

Hit me with your best shot.

I snorted and went back to the address information. If I was going to make the appointment he set up for me, I was going to need to hustle.

Ninety minutes later, I walked into a fabulous shop in the center of Rodeo Drive. The other women in the store were slender Amazons, and I felt kind of sloppy in my yoga pants and sports pullover. I pushed my hair back behind my ears and wandered over to a woman behind a glass counter.

"Hi, I'm looking for Xandra."

"She's busy with Natalie Portman right now, you'll have to come back later," the woman replied without looking up from her magazine.

"I'm under the impression that she should be expecting me. Josh Bowen made the appointment."

That made the woman pause and look up at me. Well, she looked me up and down and wrinkled her nose slightly. I didn't try to stand up straight and I didn't slump. I wasn't going to let her see that she was making me feel like a cell under a microscope.

"Well then, that's different. Please follow me. Would you like anything to drink—water, coffee, wine?"

"Um, water. Water sounds nice."

She nodded then led me up a spiral staircase to a walled-off parlor and saw me settled on a bright white leather sofa. She stalked off and returned seconds later with a heavy plastic bottle of water.

"She'll be with you in a moment. Let me know if there's anything you need."

"Thank you."

She didn't acknowledge that, just slinked off to the counter where I'd found her. I waited alone for a few minutes, sipping the water, tapping around on my phone.

This gala was a terrible idea. I made the mistake of telling Josh I didn't have a dress and he made an appointment for me at Filigree, I texted both Crystal and Shereen.

I was disappointed by their response.

Go girl! Live it up, you don't know what I would do for an appointment at Filigree. If you get to work with Xandra, I'll die from jealousy, Shereen gushed.

You're not paying, enjoy it. But remember, just because he's buying you a dress, he isn't entitled to any physical stuff, Crystal replied.

I'd been hoping for more actual support. Thanks for nothing.

Before I could think of anything else to say, a gorgeous woman with bright red lipstick swept into the room. She flipped a thick black braid over one shoulder and said, "Are you ready to get to work?"

I blinked, not really sure what to say. "Um...maybe?"

"Ah, how silly of me. I should back up. I'm Xandra, and you must be Odie, Josh's little friend. Now I hear you're going to the gala and you don't have a dress yet. That's perfect because we're going to get you built for the gala from the ground up. Any questions?"

"Several."

She laughed uproariously and sat down on the sofa next to me. "If it'll get this appointment moving along, you can ask two. I squeezed you in as a favor for Josh, but Angelina Jolie simply cannot be kept waiting, and she'll be here in two hours. But if it takes longer than two hours, that's fine. I'm used to working on multiple projects at once; you know how hectic award season can be."

"You think it's going to take more than two hours for me to get a dress?"

"Honey, depending on what we need to do, you may go from here to the gala!"

She saw the look on my face and slapped her knee. "I'm kidding, I'm kidding. But it can take a while. We have snacks for when the consultation goes a little long. We just call for one of the shop assistants and she'll come back here with whatever we want."

"This is too luxe."

"Honey, it's not your dime. The Bowens have the money, God love 'em. If they're willing to blow it on a dress for you, I would sit back and enjoy it."

"So I've been told."

"So let's stop sitting around and get started. Now, you're kind of athletic but you're not mannish or anything. We can have fun with this. But we'll stay away from halter tops."

I started rolling my shoulders nervously before protesting, "Is this how you're going to talk for the whole appointment?"

"Do I need to sugar-coat things for you?" she said, quirking one eyebrow.

"I just don't need any help feeling self-conscious before I go to a fancy party. Now can we get a dress and get going already?"

When Xandra smiled, she revealed a small gap in her perfectly white teeth. "Ahh, you're feisty. I can see why Josh likes you. I think we have something for you in burgundy."

She called into the back room and a second later there was a long, sleek burgundy dress on a hanger in front of us. I was skeptical until I noticed that the bottom of the dress had a mermaid skirt of pearl-studded tulle. Xandra waited for me to stop drooling before ushering me into a dressing room. Before I could ask, she threw over the perfect underthings and I was surprised by how well she guessed my measurements.

"How long have you been doing this?" I called.

"Since Esperanza and I were putting on plays in preschool," she said, her voice growing distant. "I'm going to the front to pick out a couple of accessories. When you're ready for a zip, come stand out here. Nobody's going to come in without knocking."

I did as she asked and came out to stand in the empty room. A moment later, she was back with a fur capelet and a pair of shoes.

"No," I said, not taking my eyes off of the fur capelet. There was no way I was wearing fur.

People-pleasing didn't occur to me when it came to matters of conscious. Fashionistas could call it ethical fur, green fur, or free-range fur, but it was all animal cruelty in my book. Besides, I ran a dog rescue, I couldn't run around wearing a fur coat like some demented Cruella de Vil.

Xandra rolled her eyes. "Just try it."

"I won't wear fur," I said, fighting the urge to stomp my foot.

"The effect of the dress is ruined. I'll see if I can find an interesting necklace instead. Stay still, my apprentice is coming in to do your hair and makeup."

"What? No, the gala isn't for hours and I need to get to work."

I wasn't liking how this appointment was going at all, but Xandra just snorted and set the shoes in front of me. "You're wearing a Filigree original to a major Los Angeles event. I'm not letting you out of here without perfect eyebrows."

She flounced off and I shook my head at my reflection in the mirror. What had I gotten myself into?

Chapter 16

When Xandra called and informed me that she would be bringing Odie to the Getty Center, I tried to argue. I had planned on picking Odie up from Filigree and using the ride to the museum as my opportunity to bring her up to speed on the event. Odie was going to the gala with me to scope out donors; I owed it to her to at least try to point her toward likely candidates.

Xandra had only told me to meet them by the statues near the main entrance at seven. I arrived early and walked the grounds of the museum. Esperanza had loved it here—she would take Victor and me all the time when we were younger. I didn't care much for the museum, but I was oddly at ease standing among the statues. They weren't statues dedicated to Esperanza, but to me, they might as well have been. My phone dinged and I looked down.

A banner notification across my phone's screen asked me to confirm my hotel reservation for the night. I sighed. I was probably overplaying my hand, but I couldn't get that kiss in the coffee shop out of my mind. Before I could talk myself out of it, I tapped the screen to confirm the reservation and walked to the main entrance.

"Josh!" Xandra squealed, throwing her arms around me. "It's been too long. I didn't know you were seeing anyone!"

I hadn't noticed her come up to me. "What?"

"Your date for the gala. You've never asked for my help for an event like this before. How long have you two been together?"

Before I could answer, Odie approached, only stumbling a little bit. She was markedly taller than I remembered her being, and I suddenly recalled Xandra's love for borderline-stripper heels. I almost asked Odie if she wanted to wear whatever shoes she brought with her instead, but Odie was already growling, "Xandra, I told you already. Josh and I are *not* together. We're just doing each other a favor. Josh, will you tell your friend here that if she doesn't stop going on about the stupid fur capelet, I am going to sic my Chihuahua army on her!"

Her violent protest made me question my decision to confirm the hotel room, but I couldn't help but smile. "Hello Odie. You look beautiful."

That just made Xandra laugh. "Oh, I know all about those kinds of favors, dear sweet Odie. But Josh is like a baby brother to me, and if you break his heart, you're going to have to answer to me. Are you sure you won't even try on the capelet? I brought it just in case…"

"NO!" Odie barked and tugged on her high blond ponytail in clear frustration.

I walked over to Odie's side and offered her my arm. "You look perfect—you don't need a capelet or anything else. Are you ready to go in?"

She smiled up at me and I smiled back. Even if she seemed a little uncomfortable in the over-the-top evening gown, she did look really good. I turned to Xandra. "Send the bill to the house. If anyone asks about Odie's outfit, we'll tell them all about Filigree, don't worry. Thank you for helping on such short notice."

Xandra probably said something, but I wasn't paying attention. I was focused on leading Odie up the steps to the entrance. She was plenty nervous about balancing in her heels. After she nearly toppled forward, I stopped her. "Odie, you don't have to torture yourself. If you want to wear your regular shoes, no one will see them under your skirt."

"No, I'm fine. I just need to get used to the height of the heels."

"If your feet hurt, you're going to have a miserable time," I said, remembering all the parties Esperanza and Xandra had attended where they came home limping with their shoes in their hands.

"Sneakers wouldn't make the right impression on potential donors. I'll be fine. I'm sure we'll be sitting half the time anyway."

Right, she had agreed to come with me for a reason. She didn't come here because she was madly in love with me. I bet she hadn't thought twice about that kiss at the coffee shop. I really had overplayed my hand with the hotel room. But there was no harm in hoping. I looked back at Odie and imagined the dress crumpled on the floor and how that blond hair would feel if I buried my face in it. When I felt a certain amount of movement below the belt, I forced myself to think of something decidedly unappealing. It wouldn't do to get my hopes up. I had to get through the gala before I could even consider asking her to the hotel.

"Josh?" Odie was staring at me expectantly.

I hadn't realized we had stopped in front of the doors.

For a horrifying moment I imagined that she could read minds, but I forced myself to play it cool. "Yes?"

I guess my easiness must have needled her further. "Is there some reason we're hovering in the doorway?"

I lied because there was no way I could tell her the truth. "No, I was just thinking about the last time I was here with my sister."

Odie nodded. "I'm sorry. I can't imagine what you're going through. But for what it's worth, you clean up pretty nicely. The satin shawl collar is very James Bond."

That was a good save. It took some self-restraint not to turn and kiss her. That was just about what every man wanted to hear when he put on a tuxedo. I settled for laughing and pulling her inside the museum. "That's the nicest thing anyone's ever said to me. I'll try not to let it get to my head."

She trailed a finger along my arm and looked at me with a small smile. "If you're patient and play your cards right, I may have a few more compliments for you yet."

I inhaled sharply and looked around for a distraction. I needed to introduce her to my father and then some potential donors. I couldn't invite her to the hotel room before that, tempting as it was. The main hall was gorgeous, but that wasn't exactly new. The same paintings and sculptures I was used to seeing with Esperanza were still there, but the bars and tables of food were a new and welcome addition.

While I was craning my head to try to spot my father, I thought I felt her pull back. I squeezed her hand and leaned in close. "How're you doing?"

"We just walked in the door. I'm doing all right. So where are we headed?"

"I thought I'd swing by and introduce you to my dad."

She frowned and I shrugged. "We'll just get it out of

the way and then you can go mingle and find some donors."

She smirked. "Are we sure that won't get me thrown out of the party?"

"If networking was enough to get you thrown out of a fundraiser, there would be no one here but the bartenders. And maybe not even them."

She snorted and gestured to her right. "Is that them over there? Shall we go say hello, then?"

We cut to the front of the receiving line. There was no mistaking the huffing of society women and their blustering husbands, but they weren't going to cause a scene. My father's intolerance for drama was well-known. It was one of those little things that I liked to take advantage of when I could.

My father was wearing a particularly striking white tuxedo suit with black satin accents similar to those on my tux, but I don't think I could have pulled off the supercilious arched eyebrow thing quite like he could. Lana was wearing a brown evening gown shot through with teal green accents. It looked like they hadn't coordinated at all, and I could just imagine how that irritated my father. Maybe we should have waited in line...but we were there and I was the one who had to step forward and make introductions.

"Dad, Lana, I'd like you to meet Odie." I smiled and took Odie's hand to draw her closer to the conversation.

My father nodded his head and held out a hand to her. "Kendall Bowen. I'm happy you could come, Odie."

She shook his hand. "Thank you for extending the invitation."

"I hope we can let bygones be bygones about the grant luncheon. Josh told me that you were wrongly disqualified, but by the time he told me, the grant had already been awarded to another worthy organization," he said, unblinking, watching for Odie's reaction.

If I hadn't been standing right next to her, I would have missed the small sigh that escaped her before she smiled brightly. "Of course, apology accepted."

A photographer popped up at the perfect moment. He didn't ask if we wanted our picture taken—we just saw a flash, and he was off. Lana caught my eye and we both had to fight not to grin as we saw my father open and then close his mouth a couple of times. I was actually going to crack open a couple local magazines later to see if that picture popped up anywhere. Finally, he nodded and turned to greet the next person in the receiving line.

I gave Odie a smile and a thumbs up as Lana leaned in to whisper, "Well done, girl. I can see Mary Agatha's spirit in you. How's the old girl doing?"

Odie gave Lana a brief hug. "She's the picture of health. Thank you for asking, ma'am."

"Oh, please, there's no need for any of that ma'am business here. Call me Lana. I love your dress."

"Thank you. Xandra kitted me out. I'm supposed to tell people it's a Filigree original. But I've never seen anything like yours, it's really spectacular."

"Kendall's a little put out by the fact that it clashes with his suit, but I told him what I was wearing and even offered to find a matching tux for him."

I think I heard my dad scoff, but it was hard to tell over the string quartet that had started playing in the corner of the room.

"I've got to say hello to some of the other guests," Lana said. "You two kids have fun. If you need anything, don't hesitate to track me down. And say hello to your granny for me, honey."

Lana turned to greet the couple my dad was talking to, and I led Odie to a quieter part of the museum.

When we were alone, she stretched and said, "Well, that wasn't too bad."

"You were a champion. I think my father may even respect you after that exchange." I was being absolutely sincere there—it was rare that I saw anyone get the better of him like that.

"I won't hold my breath. So is now a good time to scope out some donors or volunteers?"

Right, that was one of the reasons why she was here. What insanity had prompted me to get a hotel room? I had to hide my disappointment. "It's as good a time as any. Do you want me to come with you?"

Odie paused for a moment before shaking her head. "I need a few minutes to focus. Can I catch up with you in ten, maybe fifteen minutes?"

"Of course."

Odie gave my hand a squeeze and wandered into the crowd. While I watched her go, I saw Victor make his entrance in a black tuxedo with a blood-red vest. He surveyed the room and made a beeline for me. I could feel the heat of at least a dozen women's gazes on us, but that was normal for these kinds of events. What was unusual was how little it bothered me this time.

He whispered as he shook my hand, "Josh, I saw your better half talking up some octogenarian with ear-hair. What'd you do, man?"

I guffawed. "Nothing, she's talking up donors for the Rescue. That was one of the ways I convinced her to come with me."

"What does Uncle Kendall think of that?"

"Does it matter? He won't throw her out. That'd be too much of a scene for something as innocuous as networking with other guests. Besides, you should have heard her take him down a peg. It was the politest thing I've ever heard, but the look on my dad's face was amazing."

Victor bobbed his head. "I'm sure. But hey, is that Naomi over there?"

I glanced over to where he was looking and felt mildly sick to my stomach. Naomi was talking with Odie and one other man. Odie was smiling and laughing, but Naomi had a familiar, calculating gleam to her eyes. I didn't like the look of it so I cut a quick path to their side of the room.

"Naomi! So good to see you again. Is this your fiancé?" I said, giving Naomi a quick hug and offering a hand to the man standing next to her.

"Josh—" I heard Victor hiss, but it was too late.

Naomi giggled. "No, this is my boss. Josh, have you met Mr. Isaac Archambault of Archambault Ventures?"

I almost swallowed my tongue out of shock. *How could I make such a fool of myself?* I was supposed to pitch my life's work to this guy and he would probably never take me seriously after a miserable gaffe like that. So I did the only thing I could think of. I cleared my throat and said. "No, I don't believe so, but I have had the pleasure of talking to your secretary."

That made Mr. Archambault smile. "Yes, she was so excited by the prospect of your startup and insisted that I come to the gala to meet you."

Victor started to say something, but Odie beat him to it. "I think that's a photographer coming this way, should we do a picture together?"

Naomi looked at her with a curled lip but Mr. Archambault smiled. "That's a great idea. Josh, your date here is fascinating. I didn't know Los Angeles had a problem of too many abandoned Chihuahuas."

The photographer came around and took several

pictures. Once he finished, our group split up to mingle. After we were out of earshot of Mr. Archambault, I sighed. "I made an ass of myself, didn't I?"

Victor slapped his head in his hands but Odie shook her head. "No, I think we managed to limit the damage. There's no accounting for what your friend will say, but he seemed affable enough, even after you stuck your foot in your mouth."

Victor looked back and forth. "I'm glad one of us is optimistic here. If he funds the Nacho-Copter, I'll donate two grand to Purse Dog Rescue."

"I'll hold you to it."

He swept off to greet a group of women with obvious spray tans and very fake boobs. We watched him schmooze and charm them all for a second before I said, "If we can get the funding we need for the Nacho-Copter, we might be able to convince him to take one of your rescues yet."

Odie bumped my shoulder. "Come now, don't tease."

"I'm serious. I just need to figure out how to get some investors to fork over some real cash."

"I rather like having Diego at your house for the moment."

"Oh, why's that?"

"So I'll have an excuse to keep in touch with you after this night is over."

I had to stop myself from smiling too widely. "Keep talking dirty like that and I may end up dragging you back to my hotel room by that pretty ponytail of yours."

"Say the right words and I'll race you there."

I looked her straight in the eyes. "Pizza."

She swallowed and I thought she almost nodded, but then she held out an arm to the party. "But there's so much here, surely we don't need to get pizza in the hotel room."

"All right, if you say so. But now I'm going to take you past the catering stations."

I took her arm in mine and guided her around the perimeter of the room. We passed a couple of carving stations, an impressive array of fruits and vegetables, and several trays of appetizers and side dishes. There wasn't a scrap of anything I was remotely interested in eating right now.

When we'd made the full circle, I turned to her again and saw she looked similarly unenthused by the spread. I inclined my head. "So what do you think? Eat here or get delivery at the hotel?"

She put one hand on her hip. "That depends on your answer to my question."

"That is?"

"Pepperoni or meat lovers?"

I didn't have to think about my answer at all. "True love conquers all. Didn't anyone ever tell you that?"

She picked up her skirt and started running. It wasn't hard to catch up with her in those heels, and we trotted out the door without a word to anyone.

As the valet pulled my car around, something occurred to me. "My dad's going to have a fit over that exit."

"He can bite me," she said, kicking off her shoes and carrying them in her hands.

I pressed a kiss to her lips and whispered, "I'd really rather he didn't. That would color our whole night in a way I'd prefer it didn't."

Chapter 17

ODIE

As the sun beamed through the window, I tossed and turned to try to steal a few more minutes of sleep before the dogs started pestering me to go outside. I rolled over and found myself pressed up against something considerably larger than a dog. Josh let out a contented sigh and pulled me closer to him. He was so warm and cozy, it was tempting to draw myself closer to him and fall back asleep. But I had work today.

I looked around the hotel room and saw our clothes neatly laid over the desk chair in the corner of the room. My underwear was nowhere to be seen, but that was right —I had left those in my clothes bag when we left Filigree. I blushed at the thought, but then felt kind of silly. I hadn't planned on falling into bed with him after the gala, but I'd deliberately chosen not to wear anything under my dress from the waist down. But that kind of unfounded optimism had paid off...kind of like Josh booking this hotel room.

Shit, I hoped he didn't think I was easy for giving out like this. It was just...he'd just looked so damn good last night, and we were having so much fun talking and eating pizza, I think I might have been the one to drag him into bed. What could I say? It had been a little while since I'd been into a guy like this, and I was ready for some action. We must have gone like three or four rounds last night, so it was probably safe to say that he was into it too. But I couldn't get ahead of myself.

I brushed some hair out of my mouth and tried to decide what I was going to do now. It was only a Thursday, and there was plenty of work at the Rescue—more than Tuesday, because I'd ended up taking yesterday off to play dress-up. I still hadn't found the money to keep Crystal around, and I wasn't sure when I was going to do that with all the other work that had to be done. I must have sighed louder than I realized, because I felt Josh's hand rub up and down my arm.

Rather than get up and get dressed to go home, I let myself lie back in bed for a few minutes. Josh was blinking awake next to me, and he smiled when he saw me looking at him.

"Hey, gorgeous. How'd you sleep?" he said, his voice a little rough.

"After round four, I was out. You?"

"It was hard sleeping next to you. You kick in your sleep."

I paused, waiting for him to laugh, but he didn't smile any more than he had before. Finally, I said, "Really? I would know by now if I kick."

He shook his head. "Sorry, gorgeous, I have some nasty bruises from last night. I almost went to sleep in the bathtub, but I didn't want to give you the wrong idea when you woke up."

I just stared at him in shock. I was in my late twenties, and I had been in a couple of semi-serious relationships. Someone would have told me already if I did that.

"I—I do not!" I huffed and rolled away from him, pulling the comforter with me.

That made him laugh and I felt his hand snake underneath the comforter. "You do, though, but I wouldn't trade it for anything. I never would have guessed you were so wild."

His hand traced the line of my legs lightly and I kicked away because it tickled. When I realized what I had done, I laughed with him. "You did that on purpose!"

"Never. I just can't get enough of touching you, that's all."

The room started heating up, but I took a look at the clock and groaned. "No, no, it's like eight o'clock and I haven't been at work since Tuesday. No, I need to go."

I got up and grabbed a chocolate-covered strawberry from the table by the bed. There was still a little bit of champagne left in the bottle, but the pizza was totally gone. That was too bad, because leftover pizza would have been the perfect finish for a date like this. The strawberry was nice, though. I especially liked the way Josh's pupils dilated when I took a bite. If this was going to be a repeat event, I definitely had some ideas for next time.

He stretched languidly and I all but started panting at the sight of the lean muscle that covered his chest. I headed for the bathroom. If I was going to get out of this hotel room and go to work, I needed one very cold shower. I turned on the water and Josh joined me inside. He started massaging my shoulders, and I had to stop myself from moaning.

"Do you knock?" I said, shimmying away from him.

"Just trying to save water here...not trying to seduce you again at all." He waved a hand under the shower head and hissed, "We're going to have to do something about the temperature of this water, though. When the male anatomy is exposed to water this cold, the results are just embarrassing."

I couldn't help it, I about fell over laughing. "I'm sorry, I just have to get to work. It's puppy season—there are so many dogs to save right now!"

He drew a finger along my jaw to my lips and I was tempted to jump him right there, but he just kissed me softly. "All right, let's get you ready to save some mutts."

There was a quality to his voice that I couldn't quite identify, but I ended up laying a big kiss on him. He kissed back and wound his arms around me. When we broke apart, I couldn't help it. I knew I had a million other things I needed to do, but this man was just too delicious.

"Have you ever done it in the shower before?" I asked, stepping in and leading him behind me.

He resisted. "Never in sub-zero water. Can we turn up the heat?"

I let the water wash over me. It was freezing, but I wasn't cooling off. "What're you talking about? I'll be here to keep you warm."

He let out a growl and reached out for me. But when the water hit his arm, he swore and stepped back. "The spirit is willing but the body is not. But that's okay; we'll do this again later, right?"

I glanced at him and noticed he was holding his breath. "Definitely. The pizza was amazing. I really had a lot of fun."

To my amazement, he jumped in the shower after me. He was careful to stay out of the water's path, but he took my hand in his and raised it to his lips. "Me too. What are you doing tonight?"

"Trying to get caught up at work. I bet you have things to do too."

"Friday night, then?"

"Sure, Friday night sounds great."

He leaned over to kiss me, only to yelp when he was splashed by the cold water. I steadied him before he could fall and kissed him. The kissing turned into fondling, and then some very heavy petting, and fifteen minutes later we were both soaked through and gasping.

"Let's never do it with water that cold again," he said, shivering as he grabbed towels from a nearby rack.

"I bet I can talk you into it on Friday..." I said, wringing water out of my hair.

He bit his lip as he watched the water wash over me. "You know, I really wouldn't be surprised. Now I'm going to leave you alone in here before I forget that you need to be at work soon."

Oh right, work. I sighed and wrapped the towel around myself as he closed the door behind him. Friday couldn't come soon enough.

Chapter 18

JOSH

Friday night rolled around and Odie was supposed to come by any minute, but Victor would not leave. The meeting with Isaac was coming up soon and Victor had lost his mind. We were still working when Odie came to the front door.

"I'll leave in an hour. Maybe we can ask her to give us her opinion of the demo video and the new marketing material," Victor said as we walked to the foyer to let her in.

"You're leaving as soon as she sets foot in the house. We've been working since seven thirty this morning. There's not much more we're going to do or see almost twelve hours later."

Victor snorted and shook his head. "Just five minutes while we show her the video—"

"No. Now shut up, she can probably hear us through the door."

I opened the door and Odie was standing outside in her usual pullover and leggings. She looked much more at ease than she did in her evening gown, and I was more than okay with that.

"Hi," she said, looking from me to Victor.

I patted him on the back. "Hi Odie. Victor was just leaving."

That was when he decided to dig in his heels. "Actually, I'm just trying to wrap up some prep material for our meeting with a potential funder. Could I bug you for like five minutes of your time to get an opinion on—ow!"

I had elbowed him in the side, trying to be discreet about my eagerness to be alone with Odie. She looked at me and shook her head before smiling. "Sure, that sounds like fun. I got involved with a bunch of startups back in my programming days."

Victor led her inside and I shook my head. So much for getting her alone for a while, if ever, tonight. I followed them into the kitchen where the chef put out drinks and snacks for us while Victor got everything out of his messenger bag.

Odie took a look at the spread and whispered, "I don't suppose we could have pizza instead?"

"Maybe after we get my cousin on his way," I whispered back.

As Victor fired up his computer, he started asking questions about the gala. "I hardly remember seeing you two after Josh stuck his foot in his mouth in front of Isaac Archambault. Did Uncle Kendall have you thrown out?"

I started to laugh, but Odie elbowed me and I cleared my throat. "No, um, we left to get pizza."

Victor scoffed. "The gala had prime rib, caviar, and enough champagne to flood the entire museum. Did you guys really leave for pizza?"

Well, we weren't going to tell him the truth. "What can I say—when you need pizza, you get pizza?"

Odie started giggling and Victor shook his head in disgust. "Odie, what are you still doing here? My cousin is awful, his father is awful. I mean, sure they have your dog, but he's asleep in the mudroom. You can take him and run."

"I wouldn't say awful. Your cousin has his charms." She smiled at me and reached to squeeze my hand under the table.

"Ugh, you two are making me nauseous. Are we going to work on the Nacho-Copter or what?"

"Odie's only doing this as a favor for you; try to sound more grateful," I said, cracking open a beer and handing it to her. "Besides, the sooner we do this, the sooner you can be on your way."

Odie took a long drink of her beer before straightening up. "So do you want me to watch the video, or should I read through some of your material first?"

Victor started the video on his computer and we watched to see how she would react. Her face was expressionless as the video played and she waited until the end to ask a couple of thoughtful questions. I had a hard time concealing my surprise and admiration for the analysis packed into her comments. When she finally ran out of things to ask about the project, she crossed her legs under her and twisted a pencil through her hair to make a messy bun. It was a good look for her.

She was quiet for a minute before grinning. "Your pitch was great, I really liked it. The technical discussion was on point and I can't tell you how much I enjoyed that as a person with a startup background."

Victor didn't smile at that. "Were there any specific things you liked or didn't like?"

She twisted her watch around her wrist, thinking for a moment before answering. "The bit about the pizza business having a monopoly in the prepared food delivery business is clever, but it doesn't really build the case for your drone. I mean, it's fine business plan stuff, like something you'd find in a SWOT diagram, but I don't think you really need it in your elevator pitch."

Victor and I looked at each other with barely concealed wonder. We'd thought we were getting a layperson's opinion, but Odie was surprising us with a mind like a steel trap and a knack for strategy. Victor tapped on his laptop and I scribbled notes on a legal pad.

"All right, so we cut that out. What should we put in its place to communicate its value to restaurants?" I asked, taking off my glasses and polishing them.

"Maybe consider alternative customers besides restaurants. Maybe institutions might have more interest in the product. They'd probably have more money to invest in this kind of technology."

"What, like the military using drones to deliver rations and other vital supplies?" Victor asked, perking up.

"Sure, but it's a pain getting certified to be a government vendor. I was thinking of something a little less involved."

"But you're not going to say who you think we should be targeting instead, are you?" I groaned.

"No, Josh. This is your business—I'm not going to tell you how to run it. I'm happy to tell you what I think and I'm willing to help, but that's one of those fundamental things you need to determine for yourself."

"So institutions other than the military or the government writ large. Like fast food chains?"

"That's one, but I also think there's a demographic you're totally discounting."

"Well, it's for businesses, not really private individuals, though I suppose we could sell to them…"

"Right, and I understand that, but there are certain businesses that cater to particular demographics. Do you get what I'm saying?"

Victor snapped his fingers. "I think I get it. You're talking about like formula delivery, delivering foodstuffs for babies!"

He sounded so excited, but it just didn't sound right. It did get me thinking, though. "You're thinking about services for the elderly, aren't you?" I said finally.

"Not just the elderly, but the homebound and sick. Do you know how hard it can be for some people to go grocery shopping?" She nodded, her smile very sincere.

"So like meals on wheels but with drones? Do you think charities would be able to afford the drones?"

"The price tags are a little steep, but I was thinking there could be two ways around that problem at least."

"We could give some away to build awareness of the product and the uses for drones, but what do you see the second way being?" I asked her.

Victor slapped his hand on the desk. "We could have an alternative business model, or at least a supplemental model. Instead of just selling the drones outright, we could sell access to the fleet. That way institutions and businesses could test the service and see how to use it best without committing to a huge capital cost. Sort of pay by the sip instead of the bottle."

Odie clapped her hands. "Yes, I think you guys are onto something. Do you want me to stick around or should I let you get back to brainstorming?"

I couldn't help myself. I smacked a big kiss on her, and she kissed me right back. After a second Victor cleared his throat. "Should I leave you two alone?"

Odie pulled away and blushed. It was adorable. I ran a

hand through my hair and smiled. "No, sorry, we've got it under control."

We talked for a little while longer. Odie totally shared our excitement for the project. I almost managed to keep my hands to myself but I found myself rubbing her arm from time to time and wishing that I could drag her back to my room to have her all to myself.

"Well, I've got to run," Victor finally announced.

"Oh? Where are you going?" Odie asked, beating me to the question.

"I've got some errands to take care of. I'll talk to you tomorrow."

Once he left, I took Odie in my arms and smiled down at her. She smiled back up at me and laid a kiss on my lips. We were full-on making out when there was a knock at the door. We sprang apart and I said, "Come in."

Victor poked his head in. "Did I leave my sunglasses? Oh, right there."

Odie handed him the sunglasses and he thanked her, but not before giving me a very knowing look. Once he was gone and the door was shut, Odie giggled.

"Well, that was embarrassing."

"I know, who leaves their sunglasses lying around?"

She playfully punched me in the shoulder. "That's not what I meant."

I rubbed my shoulder. "Owwww, use your words! Are you really embarrassed?" I turned to her as I asked that question, curious as to how she really felt.

"I mean, not by us. It's just weird to be caught making out like teenagers."

I tried to hide my cringe at that. Yeah, it was a little embarrassing to be living at home. "We can head out to your place if you'd rather?"

"And have like four dogs watching our every move? That's okay, we can work with what we've got."

She got up to leave and I took her hand in mine, rubbing the pads of her fingertips. "So, when are we seeing each other next?"

"I have a lot to do, and you're busy, so should we just play it by ear?"

"You're not trying to tell me gently that you're not interested in continuing this anymore, are you?"

She shook her head. "No, no, I just really need to do something about getting some extra funding. I have an employee who really, really needs a raise and I don't have the budget for it right now. I want to keep her so I've got to do something. I just need some flexibility for the short term. I want to see you again."

She squeezed my hand and smiled at me. I squeezed back. "Text me, then?"

Chapter 19

ODIE

Granny called me on my way to work on Monday. That was unusual—she was usually so careful with her precious cellphone minutes. I hit the accept call button on my Bluetooth and was greeted by the sound of a ragged cough.

"Wow, Granny. How long have you had that cough?" I said, trying to remember the last time I went over to visit her.

Things had just been so busy between the gala and the time I was spending with Josh, not to mention all the makeup work I'd had to do around the shelter. It had probably been the better part of a week since I'd seen her last.

"It's just a head cold. I'm fine. I have an appointment with my GP on Thursday. We just haven't talked for forever and I wanted to hear about the gala."

"Right. It was a lot of fun."

"I bet. I know Lana was having a fit getting everything ready in time. Was it just gorgeous?"

"It was the Getty Center, it's never anything but gorgeous. But Lana looked good. I met Josh's father and he seems like kind of a jerk to be married to a sweetheart like her, but it was all fine."

"What about Josh's cousin, that male supermodel-looking one?"

"You would have loved his tuxedo. It was black but he had a blood-red waistcoat underneath his jacket."

She made an oohing sound but it quickly turned into a cough. When she finished coughing, I said, "Are you sure your doctor can't see you sooner? You sound kind of rough there."

"I'm fine. Like I said, it's just a head cold. So have you done anything with Josh since the gala?"

I had a hard time deciding on how to answer that question. I probably would have read more into the use of the phrase "done anything" if the question had come from Crystal or Shereen, but it wasn't totally out of the question that Granny would ask similarly prying questions.

"I went over to his house and ended up helping him with his tech startup pitch. He and Victor have some pretty cool ideas."

"And I bet they're ten times cooler after you heard them out and told them what to change."

"You're giving me too much credit."

"I've seen your work, missy, and while it may have been a few years since you were in the computer business, I know that every company you touched turned to gold."

I pulled into the parking lot and sighed. "You make me sound like Rumpelstiltskin or something. But I just pulled into the parking lot at work. Take it easy today and go to the doctor right away if you start feeling any worse."

She let out a couple of shallow coughs. "Aye, aye, captain. Have a good day at the Rescue. Tell the girls I said hi."

When she hung up, I pulled the keys out of the ignition

and headed inside. Shereen wasn't there yet but Crystal was lingering by my desk.

"Crystal? What's up—are you okay?" I said as I watched her push her curls over her ear for the fourth time in two minutes.

She turned and smiled at me with a little too much teeth. "Odie! I'm fine, I'm fine. I'm a little anxious, but I'm fine."

I threw my purse down on my desk and sat down, motioning for her to grab her chair too. "Whatever it is, you can tell me about it. I want to help."

That made her sigh pretty loudly. "And that's why I'm anxious. You're so good to us here and I'm making things difficult for you—"

I pulled a couple bottles of water out of my desk and pushed one at her. "Crystal, take a drink, relax. You're okay. I'm okay. We can deal with whatever's bugging you."

She drained her bottle of water and almost choked at the end. I pounded her back and said, "Would it be easier if you just told me in writing?"

She shook her head. "No, no, I need to do this in person."

A shiver went down my spine. I had a sneaking suspicion about what she was going to say, but I wasn't quite ready to hear it yet. "Do you want to go get coffee or something? I'm dying for a donut and some unadulterated caffeine."

When she nodded, I pulled out a piece of paper from my desk and scribbled out a note for Shereen. Then I put the note on Shereen's desk and led the charge out to my car. Crystal settled into the passenger seat and I got us on the road to the closest coffee shop.

We had gone maybe two miles when Crystal found her voice. "Um, I found another job."

We were both silent for a second. I looked at her out of the corner of my eye and saw her staring out the window, her head turned away from me. Finally, I said, "When?"

"I just got the offer letter earlier this morning. I'm sorry, but it's too good an offer to say no. I haven't accepted yet, I wanted to tell you first."

"That's very kind of you."

"I'm sorry, Odie, I know you were really trying, but you'll find another employee. Shereen may even step up."

"You're a hard act to follow. But I'm really happy for you. You should accept the offer right away."

"I will, I just wanted to ask how much time you thought was fair."

"Time?"

"Transition time. I think two weeks is standard."

"Crystal, you go when you need to go. If you need two days, two weeks, two months, we've got your back."

"You saying stuff like that makes me feel like a real shitheel. I'm sorry."

"For what? You didn't do anything wrong. You told me you needed to find another job, and I was supportive. I had hoped I could find something for you, but I also told you to start looking. I'm happy that you're getting closer to your dream."

She started sniffling as we pulled into a parking space at the coffee shop, and I leaned over and hugged her.

"You can go. Just don't lose touch, though, okay?"

She hugged me back. "Never. I'm going to volunteer as much as I can."

"I hope you do, but you need to do what it takes to make those law school dreams of yours a reality, okay?"

"Of course."

We got ahold of ourselves and stopped in for coffee. I

texted Shereen and told her that Crystal had wanted to tell me first and in person that she was leaving. I also offered to pick up a coffee for her. I grabbed a chocolate latte for me and an iced vanilla soy chai latte for Shereen. Crystal insisted on paying for all of it and even got me a brownie donut to boot.

I tried to sneak my card to the cashier but she bumped me out of the way. As I put my card away, I said, "That's really not necessary."

She handed me my donut and coffee. "Please, it'll make me feel better. You're just being so nice about it all and it's killing me."

"Did you think I would be angry?"

She shook her head. "No, no, I knew you would be supportive. You're nothing if not a people-pleaser, and that's what makes me feel guilty. You go to such lengths to make things work for everyone else, I feel like I'm really failing you by leaving the Rescue."

"You're not failing me. Pursuing your dreams isn't failing me."

"I just feel so guilty, okay—let me buy the coffee."

"Fine."

We piled back into the car and puttered back to the office. Shereen was at her desk listening to electronic dance music at top volume when we walked inside. She killed the music when we said hello and her eyes brightened at the sight of the coffee. "Aww! You guys are life savers. Crystal, Odie texted me saying you were leaving—where are you going?"

Crystal coughed and looked at me and hung her head. "I'm going to work for a logistics company. It won't be as satisfying as working at the Rescue, but it's what I need to do to get to law school."

There was a moment of quiet as we all tried to think of

the right thing to say. Shereen recovered first. "Well, we're going to miss you. Just don't forget us, okay?"

Crystal blinked several times, then took a breath and swallowed. After a second it dawned on me that she was trying not to cry. Watching her, I felt my own eyes start to water. We were all goners when we saw Shereen's tears trailing mascara and eyeliner down her cheeks. She looked a little like a soggy panda or raccoon with all the smudged black makeup. Then she got up and dragged us both into a group hug. We stood around crying and sniffling for a few minutes before breaking apart to get tissues and drink from our coffees.

"We need to have a send-off party. It won't be goodbye, but this way your time with the Purse Dog Rescue won't end in a whimper," I said once I didn't feel quite so choked up.

Through ragged breaths, Crystal managed to say, "That sounds fine."

When we got ahold of ourselves, we buried ourselves in our work. I checked my email and my jaw fell open when I saw the first email that morning. The owner of Winery de los Patos wanted to donate and sponsor our next community event. It was wonderful, it was generous, but it was a dollar short and hours too late. I couldn't tell Crystal or Shereen—I didn't want to make Crystal feel awkward. I could tell Shereen later, so I replied back, thanking the owner profusely and offering to give them a tour of the facilities at their earliest convenience.

The day went by in near silence. I took the dogs on long walks and worked with Carmencita on her leash skills. When the clock struck five thirty, Crystal and Shereen found me cleaning kennels and asked if I wanted to get something to drink.

"No, thanks, I have a couple of things that need to be taken care of. We'll have to do it some other night."

I needed some time to get ahold of myself. Everything I'd told Crystal was true—I really was happy for her, but I was just so sad to see her go. I needed to get over myself and make her exit as smooth as possible. I owed her at least that much.

My phone lit up when a telemarketer called, and I hit the reject call button, but it gave me an idea.

He answered after two or three rings.

"Josh? It's Odie."

"Odie! How're you doing? I was just thinking about you, your timing is perfect."

To my horror, I started crying. "My timing is the opposite of perfect."

"What's the matter, ba—Odie? Is there anything I can do to help?"

"No, she's found another job. She's leaving in two weeks."

"Who? Crystal?"

Hearing her name just made me cry harder. "Yeah. She's my best friend; I can barely remember running the Rescue without her."

I dissolved into tears and heard Josh sigh before saying, "Odie, I'm sorry. If I hadn't roped you into that kiss at the luncheon, my dad wouldn't have taken you out of the running for the grant and you'd still have Crystal at the Rescue."

I paused at that. He was right, but that wasn't why I was crying. I wasn't mad at him for that—I hadn't been mad at him for weeks. "Well, I mean, that may be so, but if you hadn't done that, who would have helped me with Diego?"

He laughed. "Lana is in love with that dog. Did you follow up with anyone from the gala about donating?"

I sniffed. "I've been meaning to. Things have just been so crazy here, I haven't had a chance."

"Hey, I have an idea for you. You've had a busy couple of weeks, you probably need a break. Will you come with me to the beach for a couple days?"

I sniffed again. "I can't get away right now, there's too much to do before Crystal leaves."

His tone was gentle but more firm than I liked when he said, "You're always inhumanly busy, Odie. I realize how important your work is to you, but I'm worried that you're going to get burned out. If you're swamped now, things are probably going to be much more hectic after Crystal leaves. Just take two days off with me, relax, recharge, and then go back to work with a plan. Will you at least consider it?"

"What about the Nacho-Copter? Don't you have things to do to get ready?"

"We've got it well in hand. Victor's a huge workaholic but I'll worry about him after I've taken care of you. What do you say?"

There was so much to do, I really had no business going out of town at the last minute. But I had so much fun with him, and surely I deserved a little happiness after this huge letdown. I thought aloud for a minute. "I'll need to find someone to watch the dogs while we're gone. Oh, and Granny goes to the doctor on Thursday and I really like to be there with her for doctor's appointments. Can we be back by Thursday morning, early?"

"You got it. Are you still at work?"

"Yes, but I need to go home to pack, let the dogs out, and figure out a few logistics."

"What would you say if I told you that you could bring the dogs?"

If I was being totally honest, I would say that the offer made me smile. But some facts couldn't be ignored. "I'd ask you if you were sure. I mean, I have four dogs."

"But they're all little dogs. Like Diego's size, right?"

"Yeah, close to it anyway. But there are four of them; are you sure they won't drive you crazy?"

Josh laughed. "Odie, if they make you happy, I want you to bring them. Besides, I bet they'll love the beach."

"Okay, so I still need to go home and get everything. What time were you thinking of heading out?"

"I was thinking of picking you up in about two hours?"

"Yes."

"Perfect. See you then, angel."

The line went dead and I smiled. He'd called me "angel." It was kind of funny, I never would have thought the jerk from the blind date could ever be so considerate. Or put up with four dogs willingly. I'd have to tease him about that on the trip.

Chapter 20

JOSH

When I asked Odie to come with me to the beach, I didn't tell her we were going to Esperanza's house. Well, it was our family's house; she left it to Dad and Lana but the house really hadn't changed since Esperanza left it. If I didn't need to spend so much time in Los Angeles, I probably would have moved in here with Ceviche. It was probably for the best too because Odie about had a fit when we parked in the driveway.

"You said we were going to the beach! You never said anything about a seaside mansion!" she said with an accusatory scowl.

"I'm sorry, we can find a less convenient beach house, I just thought the dogs might enjoy being able to go straight from the house to the beach," I explained as I pulled our suitcases out of the trunk and handed them to the housekeeper who stayed at the guest house year-round.

"This is too much. We're inconveniencing the housekeeper—we can carry our suitcases up to the house. I can't believe I let you talk me into this."

The housekeeper shook her head but I smiled. "Thank

you, Quincy, we don't have that much—we can get everything inside on our own."

Quincy rolled her eyes but set the suitcases down on the driveway. "If you two need anything at all, you know where to find me."

We watched the housekeeper walk back to her house and I picked up the bags. They really weren't very heavy, except for the rolling cart with all of the dogs' things—that one was about to crack at the seams. Once we had everything inside, I reached for Odie's hands and stroked the skin between her thumb and forefinger. "Angel, I wanted to give you a chance to relax. You deserve some downtime with your dogs, and this was the easiest way to do it. Can I make it up to you by ordering a pizza?"

Her stomach growled and she let out a huff. "Fine, fine—you know pizza is my weakness. Let's go."

She let all of her dogs off their leashes and they ran all over the house smelling everything. It had been a while since Ceviche had been to the beach house, but I couldn't imagine he'd be happy with the pack of mutts crisscrossing the halls. Odie made herself comfortable in one of the plush leather recliners in the living room, and a wizened three-legged dog came and sat at her feet. I picked up the dog and put him in her lap before sitting next to her. The dog growled at me and I jumped up.

"What'd I do wrong?" I asked from the wet bar in the corner of the room.

"Woz isn't a fan of being picked up by strangers. I have some treats in the cart if you want to try to bribe your way back into his good graces." Odie waved at her cart where one of her dogs was circling like a shark who smelled blood.

I poured myself a drink. Maybe inviting Odie and all four of her dogs wasn't my best idea. But Odie and the dogs were a package deal, so I just forced a smile. "Anything to tide you over until I can order a pizza?"

"What kind of wine do you have over there?"

"Well, there's nothing here in the wet bar but we can go down to the wine cellar—oh, don't look at me like that. Just come on."

She was giving me this horrified look and the dog had this smug expression, and between the two of them, it was ridiculous. I held out a hand to help Odie out of her chair and lead her down the hallway toward the kitchen. The dogs clicked along behind us but I closed the kitchen door once we were through.

"Well, that was ominous. Who's going to defend my virtue now?" she said, eying a bowl of strawberries on the counter.

"The wine cellar's this way. I just didn't want to risk losing one of the dogs in the secret passage."

"The what, now?"

I pulled on a thick cookbook on a shelf next to the pantry and the rug in front of the kitchen sink slid away to reveal a trap door. Odie's eyes bugged out and I smiled. "I know, it's ridiculous, but Esperanza had just made partner and she figured that half the joy of having a boatload of money was being able to blow it on goofy shit like this. Do you want to pick out a bottle?"

Odie eyed the trap door distrustfully. "Is it safe?"

"Safe as a kitten. I didn't know there were architects that specialized in hidden rooms and Scooby-Doo rooms, but she found the best of them. If you really don't want to come down with me, I can bring something up for you."

She snorted and was at my side in a second. "And miss the secret wine cellar? Not happening. So are you going to open the door or what?"

I pressed a kiss to her temple and bent down to lift

open the door. The motion triggered lights to flicker on in the wine cellar, and I led Odie down the short staircase. Her eyes somehow got even bigger when she saw the collection of wine in the cellar.

"Which way to the Cabernet Franc?" she breathed after taking a lap around the room.

"Good choice. Follow me."

We went to the far corner of the room and started picking through the bottles on the wall. Well, she started pawing through the collection; I stood back and watched her for a minute. Her forehead was wrinkled and I think she was even humming quietly to herself. I could hear her dogs barking, but it sounded very far away. After a couple of minutes, she turned and presented a bottle to me.

"What do you think about this one?"

I looked at it and almost laughed. The label was dominated by an enormous duck. "I'm sure it's fine, but if it tastes like the cheap wine with the giant rooster on it, I may never forgive you."

She laughed and tucked the bottle under her arm. "Oh? Well, I guess we'd better go find a bottle opener, then, because I've had wine from this vintner before and it's fantastic. I'm willing to bet it's going to be the best bottle you've ever had."

"What are you willing to bet?" I reached out a hand for hers and started petting her knuckles.

"If this is best bottle of wine you've ever tasted, we'll leave Quincy alone for the entirety of our trip. We won't bother her for a thing, including dishes."

"And what if it's just okay wine, or maybe even bad wine, what then?"

"I will…kiss it better, I guess," she said, sounding somewhat unsure, but there was a familiar quality to her voice, a throatiness that reminded me of the night of the gala.

"Can we skip the bet and go straight to the kiss? I've missed you so much, you have no idea how often I have to stop myself from calling you at crazy hours of the night."

She smiled but there was some hesitation. "It's just been a crazy day. Can we take some time and chill out?"

I felt myself blush. "Of course. You don't have to do anything you don't want to. I just wanted to let you know that I've been thinking about you."

She blushed too and leaned forward to kiss me. I let her take the lead, but I almost cried when she pulled back. "Let's collapse on the couch, kill this bottle, eat some pizza, and then we'll see where things go?"

"That works for me."

I followed her out of the wine cellar and called the closest pizza place to get delivery once we were back in the kitchen. I popped open the bottle and poured two glasses. Odie took one from me and almost drained it in one gulp.

"Are you okay?" I said, trying not to sound too worried.

"I'm fine, I just…it's been a hard day. I don't normally do that sort of thing. It was really good, though."

I took a sip of my own glass and nodded. It was one of the better wines I'd had lately. "Well, I guess we're leaving Quincy alone for this trip." I smiled and noticed Odie sigh pretty deeply. "But I want to show you something before we go sit back down. Will you get the dogs and bring them out on the back deck?"

"Sure…?"

"I'll just be a few minutes, then."

I went to the foyer where we had left our bags and pulled out a case for one of my drones. I'd brought one of my more user-friendly drones in case we had a little down-time. I pulled it out of the case and went out to the back deck.

Odie was lying on a lounge chair and her dogs were

sprawled all over her. They got up when they saw me coming, and Odie tilted her head.

"Don't tell me you brought the Nacho-Copter to the beach. Isn't the salt air bad for machinery like that?"

"No, the Nacho-Copter's back at home. It occurred to me that you helped us with the pitch for the Nacho-Copter, but I remember you saying once upon a time that you didn't see the point of drones. So I thought I should show you."

Odie groaned. "Is this going to be work?"

"It's not supposed to be. Try it, and after five minutes, if you still think drones are stupid, you never have to look at it again." I held the controller out to her.

"Can I operate it from here?" she asked, not moving from the lounge chair.

"As long as you can see, sure."

I dropped down on the ground and got the drone set up. Woz jumped down from Odie's chair and came to sniff the drone but lost interest after a few minutes.

"Do you have any dog toys?"

"Not out here, but there should be a few in the cart."

I went inside and picked through the cart until I found a small tennis ball and brought it back outside. I put the ball inside the drone's grasping claw and got it in the air. I went to sit next to Odie and showed her the controls.

"This is how you make it go forward. This makes it go backwards. If you want to go up or down, you pull the lever accordingly. When you want the grasping claw to release, hit this button," I said before handing her the remote control.

"I'm not going to crash this thing, am I?" she said, taking the remote control from me with her eyebrows raised.

"No, I put it in beginner mode—you don't have to worry about crashing it. Give it a try."

She sat up straighter and took the drone higher into the air. The dogs were all watching with rapt attention. Once she got comfortable with the controls, she sent it swooping to the left and the right and even figured out how to do front flips. The dogs were barking and wagging their tails. Odie was even smiling.

When she hit the button to release the dogs' ball from the drone, the dogs went wild. They went racing after the ball and Odie started laughing.

"Still don't see the point of drones?" I said, smiling at her.

"Okay, this is pretty fun. Where's the pizza, though? I'm dying to eat."

Right on cue, the doorbell rang. I left Odie and the dogs on the deck and got the pizza. I set everything up in the kitchen and then went back out to bring her inside. I found Odie with her phone pressed against her ear.

She was white as a sheet. When I put a hand on her shoulder, she was shaking.

"What's the matter?" I asked in a whisper.

Odie shook my hand from her shoulder but didn't answer my question. "I'll be there...as soon as I can. Tell her I'm coming. Thank you for calling me."

She hung up the phone and got to her feet, stumbling a little. I wrapped my arms around her and spoke softly. "What's the matter, angel?"

"My granny's in the hospital. I need to go to her." She had tears in her eyes as she spoke and my heart broke at the sight of her.

"We can go right now. We can ask Quincy to watch the dogs if you want to go straight there."

"No, that's all right. I'll call Crystal and she can meet us at the hospital and take the dogs home for me."

"It's no trouble. Quincy would understand—"

"No, I don't think I'm going to have time to come back here. We should just get everything back home tonight."

I nodded. There was no point in arguing; she needed to get back to Los Angeles. She wasn't going to feel better until she saw her grandmother.

"Definitely, but can I talk you into eating some pizza while we're on the road? I know how scary this must be, but trust me, some greasy comfort food will make you feel a little bit better."

She smiled, but I could see her eyes watering. "If greasy comfort food will make me feel better, then we might as well bring the whole box with us."

I squeezed her shoulder. "We can do that. I also want you to know that I'm here for you."

She sniffed and swiped at her eyes. "Thank you, Josh. I'm sorry to cut this short."

"We'll just have to pick this up another time."

We wrangled the dogs and brought them back inside. As we loaded our bags and the pizza box into the car, I asked, "Do you know what's the matter with your grandmother?"

"The damn cough was pneumonia."

"Oh, shit. But she's generally pretty healthy, right? I remember her being pretty spritely when she came by my house with Diego."

Odie settled into the car. "She is, but she's at the age where those illnesses are scary. I'm so mad I didn't make her go to the doctor sooner!"

"Odie, you can't blame yourself. Your grandmother's a grown woman."

"A grown woman who won't admit she needs help. She raised me. She's all I have left, I can't lose her!"

"Odie, you won't. She's getting help now. She's going to be fine. We're on the road, we'll be there in an hour or two. Is Crystal going to meet us at the hospital to take the dogs?"

Odie buried herself in her phone. I drove onto the interstate and was pleased by how little traffic there was on the road. We were going to make good time.

After a few minutes, Odie set her phone down and leaned her head against the window. "We just talked this morning. Why didn't I go check on her?"

"Because I talked you into a spontaneous getaway." I sighed and reached for her hand.

She took my hand and squeezed. I waited for her to say something, but she was silent.

Finally, I said, "You know your granny's not all you have left, right? You know you've got me."

She didn't answer; she didn't nod yes or no—I just heard a sniff. And that scared the hell out of me.

Chapter 21

ODIE

I hated hospitals. They always reminded me of the night I lost my parents. We were all in a car crash, my mom, dad, and I—a drunk driver hit our car. I lived, but my parents didn't make it. We were all rushed to a hospital that smelled just like this one: antiseptic and misery. Once we met Crystal and handed over the dogs, I went to the reception desk and said hello to the lady behind the counter.

She barely looked up at me. "Odessa Ferguson?"

"Yes?"

"Your grandmother's in room 534 and your friend's sitting with her. You can see her soon, but her doctor wanted to talk to you first."

I couldn't think of which friend would be sitting with her. I had only called Crystal after I'd learned about Granny. "Oh-kay."

"Take a seat and he'll come around shortly. Sir, have you been helped?" She craned around me to address Josh.

"Um, I'm with her."

The lady went back to what she was doing and we sat

down in the miserable cloth-covered folding chairs that were probably crawling with Ebola. I put my sweater down on the seat and rubbed my arms together. Hospitals were always so miserably cold, but I wasn't going to sit on the bare seat. Josh took off his jacket and draped it around my shoulders.

He sat down next to me and leaned in close. "Can I get you some coffee, maybe some tea?"

"Sure, coffee please."

"How do you take your coffee?"

"Pour enough cream and sugar in there to turn the whole thing a very pale beige."

"You got it."

He walked off and I pulled the jacket around me. Then I took out my phone and started texting Crystal. I thanked her again and told her that I was going to see Granny soon. I had just sent the text when a tall, rail-thin man in a white coat came to stand in front of me.

"Ms. Ferguson?"

I looked up at him and nodded. "Yes, sir?"

He held out a hand. "I'm Dr. Ghaisas, your grand-mother's doctor. How are you today?"

Before I took his hand to shake, I hesitated. *When was the last time he washed his hands?* I mean, doctors are supposed to wash their hands, but they're human, they make mistakes. But I couldn't afford to offend my grandmother's doctor, so I pushed past my fear of contracting some hideous bacterial disease and said, "I'm a little freaked out, thanks for asking. Can I see her now?"

"In a minute. I just wanted to talk with you first."

"How bad is it?" I breathed, lifting one hand to hover over my mouth.

"I didn't mean to alarm you. I should say first that your grandmother's really in pretty good shape for a woman in her eighties. Pneumonia can be scary, but she came in before it got too bad. Still, we have to face facts—she may not be so lucky in the future. You need to help her slow down."

"But that's never going to work—she's very active. She'd be miserable if I told her to stay home and watch soap operas."

"I'm not saying that she has to turn into a couch potato. It just seems like tai chi, gardening, and all of her other hobbies are overwhelming her. She's at the age where she just can't bounce back like she used to."

"Why are you telling me this now? Did you find something in your tests?"

"No, it's pneumonia. She'll get some antibiotics, some bedrest and lots of fluids, and she'll be fine. I just don't want her to come back here, or to any other hospital, before she absolutely has to."

"Oh, okay. So can I see her now?"

"Which activity are you going to encourage her to scale back on?"

"What do you mean?"

"She needs to do less if she wants to keep her health up. I would recommend against gardening at her age— it's too easy to lose one's balance carrying plants or lugging around garden hose."

"She's always had a garden. I've never known my grandmother without a plant."

"She doesn't have to stop gardening altogether. But maybe she can stick to just a potted plant on the windowsill?"

"I'll talk to her. She's an adult; she has full possession of her faculties. If we tell her what the deal is, she'll make the decision that will make her happiest."

There was a look on his face that told me that he didn't

believe my statement for a second. "Maybe you're right, but that would make your grandmother perhaps the most reasonable senior citizen I've ever worked with."

I stood upright as Josh walked back into the waiting room with two cups in his hands. He looked from me to the doctor and gave me a tentative smile. I smiled and nodded at him as he came forward.

"Hi there—Josh Bowen. Here's your coffee, angel, as much milk and sugar as I could stand to pour in the cup. Is there any news on Mary Agatha?"

I took the coffee cup and said, "Yes, I'm going in to see her. Thank you for the coffee. If you need to go, I understand."

He paused. "Do you want me to go?"

"I really need to be there for my grandmother right now. And I know you have that presentation coming up. Can we call each other later?"

I saw his lips thin, and then he forced a bright smile onto his face. "Sure, that sounds great. Well, tell Mary Agatha I said hello and…yeah. Take care, Odie."

I shrugged off the jacket he lent me and handed it to him. It had an oddly final feeling to it, and I noticed that he swallowed hard as he took it over his arm. He smiled and turned around and walked out of the waiting room. The doors wafted shut behind him and I turned to Dr. Ghaisas. "Are we ready?"

"He could have come too…" the doctor started to say, before trailing off. "Yes, right this way, please."

We went down a corridor that bent around a couple of times. There were old people everywhere. Some were lying in bed hooked up to machines, looking for all the world like corpses, and there were others who walked and sat upright but looked as hollow as dolls. I hated the thought of Granny getting any older. I mean, she couldn't get any younger, but the idea of her turning into either of those types made me want to curl up under a rock and die. Finally, we came to room 534 and Dr. Ghaisas knocked on the door frame.

"Knock, knock. Hi again, Mary Agatha. I've brought Odie to say hello."

Granny's voice was a little raspy as she said, "Dr. Ghaisas, you know how to improve a hospital visit. Hello Odie. Did I scare you?"

I heard a familiar laugh. I had to blink a couple of times to make sure I wasn't seeing things. *How did Shereen get here?*

The sight of Granny in bed looking more ashen than I could ever remember made me cry, despite my best efforts not to. "You about gave me a heart attack! You told me you were feeling bad this morning—why didn't you just come straight here instead of making an appointment with your doctor for Thursday? You could have died!"

My grandmother just snorted. "I wasn't feeling confused when I talked to you this morning. I only realized it was serious at lunch when I was talking on the phone with Lana. She told me I had just asked when the nineteen forty-nine Macy's Thanksgiving Day Parade was supposed to be on television. Lana came around and brought me to the hospital, and Dr. Ghaisas has been patching me up since."

"Thank God for Lana," I said, sinking into a chair next to Granny's bed and trying to push any thought of Lana's stepson from my mind.

I turned to Shereen in the chair on the other side of the bed. "What brought you here?"

"Crystal texted me. She didn't want your granny sitting

alone while you were on your way. I came straight to the hospital."

"Thank you so much. I hope we didn't pull you away from anything?"

"Not at all, I was just going to my uncle's house to play with the kittens. They're so cute, you would die."

Granny perked up. "Kittens?"

Shereen pulled out her phone and brought up pictures of the kittens. They were pretty adorable, and the mother looked so much healthier than when we first found her.

Once we were finished cooing over the pictures, Granny turned to me and grinned. "Besides your near heart attack, how was your day?"

I sighed. She would make light of my reaction to her being hospitalized. "It was a pretty mixed bag. Crystal got another job and she's leaving in two weeks, but I saw Josh. He brought me here, actually."

"Oh, I didn't pull you away from a date, did I?" Granny asked, somehow managing to sound both disappointed and hopeful at the same time.

"Don't worry about it, we can pick it up some other time." I must have been crazed from the events of the day, because during normal times I wouldn't have given my grandmother even that much to gloat over.

Her eyes sparkled, and while I dreaded the inevitable teasing, I was relieved to see her so engaged. "Oh, that's wonderful. I'm sorry I worried you and made you cut your date short. I just didn't think I could wait for my doctor's appointment."

Dr. Ghaisas nodded. "I'm so glad you came. It's better not to give these things a chance to really sink into your lungs. Now, I know you're concerned, Ms. Ferguson, but we can't wear your grandmother out talking. So, Mary Agatha, when you feel your voice getting scratchy, I want you to stop talking and drink some tea. Maybe take a nap. I've got to see to some other patients. Please use the buzzer if you need anything."

He swept off and Granny giggled. "He's kinda cute. Reminds me a little of your grandfather."

"Oh, how so?" I said, curious. I had never met my grandfather. He'd died when my mother was in high school, but Granny loved telling me stories about him.

"Just the way he carries himself. He has a habit of pushing his glasses up the bridge of his nose; your grandfather was constantly having to do the same. But I'm curious to hear more about what you've been up to with Josh. Spill, sister."

I snorted. There was no way I was telling my grandmother, of all people, the details of my evening. "We were at the beach."

"At the beginning of the week? Didn't you say that Crystal had just put in her notice?"

"Yes, but Josh was convinced that a short getaway would give me time to relax and get centered before things really get busy before she leaves."

"That's pretty sensible. So what hotel were you going to stay at while you were at the beach?"

I paused, certain she wasn't asking what it sounded like she asked. Then Shereen snorted and I blushed. "Um... his family has a nice beach house. It worked out, I got to bring my dogs. But we were going to stay in different rooms."

That probably wasn't true, but I felt compelled to protect my granny. Shereen shook her head but Granny didn't notice.

"Odessa Jane Ferguson, I've seen their regular house. Tell me what their beach house looked like and don't spare any details."

I sagged against the back of the chair in relief. "The house was insane. His sister had a wine cellar put in—"

"Wine cellars aren't that big of a deal."

"I'm sorry, how many people do you know who can pull on a book and open a hidden entrance to a wine cellar below their kitchen?"

She grinned. "Did you see anything else besides his trap door?"

If she hadn't been in the hospital bed, I would have smacked her on the arm.

"Granny!"

"I'm a pitiful old woman in the hospital—I worry about what's going to happen to you once I'm gone. So would you say that things are getting pretty serious between you and Josh now?"

I couldn't help lightly slapping her arm. "Granny! We've only been on a handful of dates!"

"So after Bible study this week I'll just speculate with Lana about the odds of a fall wedding for you two?"

Blushing didn't even begin to describe the flaming feeling of my cheeks, so I tried to change the subject. "Do you think they'll let you out in time?"

"Odie, you know I go to Bible study come hell or high water."

I groaned at the pun and Granny laughed and laughed until she started coughing like she was hacking up a lung.

She took a long drink of water out of a glass on her bedside table and then switched to a cup of hot tea. She shivered when she drank the tea and made a face. "This decaf tea is just the worst. I don't know why they don't keep any decent tea around here."

"I'll smuggle some Twinings in for you tomorrow."

"That's sweet of you. So did Dr. Ghaisas talk to you about my need to slow down a little?"

"He talked about it more like it was scaling back instead of slowing down."

"But it's slowing down all the same. He's right, I know. I ache a little bit more after every day of gardening. Tai chi's not so bad, but it's taught by a senior citizen for senior citizens."

"But what about your garden?"

"I guess we can let the annuals fade out and the perennials will take care of themselves if we stop fussing over the soil and everything. Weeds can fill the flower bed, it's just as well."

"Granny, it kills me to hear you talk that way."

"But that's the way it has to be. But I'd like to try container gardening instead. I mean, if I can't play around in the dirt, it'd be nice to have at least something I can hang on to."

"Maybe we can dig up some of the plants in your garden and put them in pots. That way you don't have to start totally from scratch."

"That's a good idea. That way it's like I get to hang on to some of my hard work."

"You're bumming me out talking like that, Granny."

"Well, I'd like to talk about you and Josh but you're being very puritanical."

I couldn't keep dancing around the truth. "I blew him off once he got me here. I just have so much to do, and look what happened in one day, for Pete's sake! Crystal gets a new job, you get pneumonia, and what am I doing? Screwing around! I know better. I have more important things to do and I'm going to get my priorities straight now."

Granny put her hands on her cheeks. "I think your priorities are fine! Oh, that makes me so happy to hear that you and Josh are so well-suited for each other. You know,

I'm fine with scaling back. I'll do whatever I have to in order to stick around for your wedding day."

I smacked her shoulder gently. "Well, when you talk that way, that's just going to make me push the wedding date back indefinitely. There is no wedding date. I don't have any prospects."

"Um, you brought your four dogs to a private beach house with a man who planned the trip at the drop of a hat to try to make you feel better. I'd say you have at least one prospect."

"But we're not going to get married. We're probably finished. He got his date, I got the foster for Diego, our professional relationship can start wrapping up now. It's just as well, I have so much I need to do. I need to find someone to pick up Crystal's slack before she leaves."

"Why do I get the feeling that you're throwing yourself into work to avoid other things?"

Shereen had been quiet for most of our conversation, but she started snickering at Granny's question.

I started blushing again so I cleared my throat and said, "I don't know what you're talking about."

"Oh, sure you don't. But listen, kid, my throat is beginning to get a little scratchy. I think I'm going to try to choke down the rest of this disgusting tea and wash it down with water. Then I'm going to take a long, luxurious nap on this flimsy hospital mattress. Can you and Shereen see yourselves out?"

Shereen got up. "Feel better, Mary Agatha. Odie, if you want to take tomorrow off, I already talked to Crystal and we can manage the office. Take it easy, you two."

"Thanks, Shereen. If you need anything at all, call me."

Shereen nodded and left. I got up and straightened my sweater before heading toward the door. "I was expecting you to walk me to the door, Granny. I'm hurt that you would let the door slam in my face like this."

"You're lucky you're on the other side of the room or I'd smack you."

"I love you too, Granny."

Chapter 22

JOSH

I couldn't fall asleep. I had a huge headache and Ceviche was hogging the bed. When sunlight shone through the curtains, I checked my phone. There was nothing from Odie, but like six messages and three calls from Victor.

The most recent message said, *Talked to Lana, I'm on my way.*

With a groan, I got out of bed and cracked my back. Ceviche meowed and tried to lead me to the door to get breakfast. I opened the door so he could bug the chef instead while I took a quick shower.

I had barely finished dressing when Victor charged into my room. "So the beach house...did you have fun for like the five minutes you were there?"

Ceviche came back into the room and meowed. I pulled a chair out of the guest room for Victor and set it up next to my desk. Before Victor could sit, Ceviche jumped into the chair. I picked him up, indifferent to his clawing protests, and set him on the floor. I scratched behind his ears and he purred for a minute before swatting at my hand. Then he hopped up on the bed and proceeded to lick himself.

"Pretty good until she got a call saying her grandmother was in the hospital."

Victor dropped into the chair. "Oh, God, is she all right?"

"She has pneumonia. I don't know too much more. Odie sent me away after I brought her coffee."

"Ah, she's probably just a little freaked out. I don't blame her."

"Yeah, but it was weird. It was like a switch was flipped and suddenly she was all distant and noncommittal. Like she gave me the whole 'you're busy, I'm busy' thing and left things in the air."

"She's under a lot of pressure. You know what it's like caring for a sick relative."

"Yeah, but I don't remember flaking out on people or pushing them away."

"Seriously, dude?"

Victor did that arched eyebrow thing I usually associated with my dad so well, it was almost terrifying.

I held up my hands. "All right, maybe I was a little remote."

"You ignored me for like three weeks. Just go easy on her. Maybe give her a little space to get things figured out."

"But we just had so much fun, and I know that I could help her with her grandmother. I mean, I don't know how bad things are, if they're even bad, but I know what it takes to help a sick person. I'd gladly help."

"And that's really nice of you, but if she doesn't want the help, you've got to back off for a while."

"I miss her."

"But didn't you see her like last night?"

"Yeah, but I don't know. We were having so much fun and I was beginning to think that maybe we really had a shot with each other. She's just so amazing, you know?" As I said it, I felt foolish. She'd totally brushed me off, but here I was pining for her like a loser teenager who couldn't take a hint.

Thankfully, Victor didn't do that eyebrow thing again, but he was laughing at me. "You're giving up really easy, you realize that, right?"

"I can take a hint, I know when I'm not wanted. It's too bad, though, I don't remember the last time I felt like this about a woman."

"Not even Naomi?"

"Why'd you bring her up, man?" I dragged a hand down and over my face at the memory of pulling Odie in for a kiss in front of the college crush who'd scorned me.

"I mean, you were hung up on her for a long time—her rejection destroyed your confidence for years. You haven't even tried to date outside of the occasional date Lana and your father have bullied you into. This thing between you and Odie is big; I just want to make sure I understand how big."

"It's bigger. I think Odie really wants me instead of you. Even though I had my reservations in the beginning."

"Why are you so convinced that I'm every woman's type? Of the two of us, you're the one who's been on a date more recently."

He said it in a joking sort of way but he sounded almost jealous. I straightened my shirt cuffs. "Women are drawn to you like a magnet. I only went on a date because Dad and Lana twisted my arm. If you want to go on a date so badly, you could just let Lana set one up for you."

"You know that's not my style."

"Then I guess we'll just be forever alone."

"That's awfully self-pitying. You like Odie, and I saw the way you ran out of the gala together."

"Shut up!"

"You had fun; you really like her and you're freaked out that she's putting the brakes on things because she's worried about her grandmother. Is that about right?"

"Basically."

"So stop worrying about all of that. You're going to see her and talk to her again sometime soon—you still have the dog that her adoption agency is in charge of. For now, try to focus on the presentation. We can't embarrass your dad."

"Right. I haven't talked to him since I told him I was going to the beach house and bringing four dogs with me. Do you think he's pissed?"

"He might not be too impressed. Let's finish this presentation and see if he wants to look it over. He'll appreciate the offer."

"Or he'll ask why we're wasting his time."

"You know, for an entrepreneur, you're awfully pessimistic. Negative, really."

"I'm realistic. I know my dad, okay?"

"Okay, fine, forget about your dad for the moment. What can we do to fix the presentation to make them stop laughing us out of the room?"

"Make our pitch like five hundred percent less corny?"

"Haha, but it's a food delivery system. Your pun game is just too strong for this business."

"Thank you. So maybe you should do all of the talking. Women really respond to you."

"Yeah, too bad there aren't more of them in the venture capital space."

We both let out an uncomfortable chuckle.

"So what are we going to do to fix the presentation?"

"Maybe if we had someone to practice on. Like if we know where they start to laugh us out, maybe we can spin around and fix it before we get shown the door."

"That's a pretty good idea. Who could we enlist to be our pretend audience?"

We both turned to Ceviche and he started to make a hacking sound. I set him down on the floor. "You've already coughed up a hairball on my comforter once this month, I'd really rather not have to burn it."

"Really, though, are you going to be okay?" Victor asked, eyeing me with all seriousness.

"I'll be fine."

"Okay, man."

Chapter 23

ODIE

I came to the office Wednesday morning with a box of donuts and a travel carton of coffee. Shereen winced at the sight of the box, but Crystal grabbed a stack of paper napkins and plates out of the kitchen cupboard and helped herself to a bear claw.

"Do you know how many carbs are in those things?" Shereen eyed the sugar-glazed pastry with horror.

"I don't know. Do you know how many chemicals are in the lipstick you slather on your lips every morning? Or how many carbs are in each wear?" Crystal shot back.

"That doesn't make any sense."

"Over the course of an average woman's lifetime, she'll eat about six pounds of lipstick. How many calories are in six pounds of lipstick?"

Shereen closed her mouth and took a cup of coffee and poured five packets of sucralose into it.

"So how's Granny doing?" Crystal prompted.

"She's good. She should be able to get out of the hospital tonight."

"I'm so relieved. Now that she's better, you can give Josh a call." Shereen grinned.

"I don't think I will. I have so much to do getting Granny settled, writing grant applications, and finding someone to pick up Crystal's work. I just don't have the time for a relationship."

Shereen's grin vanished and her forehead wrinkled more than I'd ever seen before. "But you've been so much happier lately…"

"Yeah, but it was just fun. It wasn't anything serious."

"Why are you so against having a relationship? You say you don't have time, but we know that's not true."

"No, no, it's true. I need to buckle down and find someone who can fill Crystal's shoes, preferably before she leaves. I don't know how I'm going to find anyone on such short notice, especially someone who can do as much work as Crystal for the pittance I'm able to pay employees. Even if I do find someone, I have a sneaking suspicion that I'll be picking up plenty of slack while they get their bearings here."

Crystal hung her head. "I'm sorry, Odie—"

"No, you don't have to be sorry. I totally understand. I want you to go to law school, I want you to be successful, but I am going to miss you. It just kills me that I couldn't find a way to keep you here."

Shereen set her cup of coffee down on the table with a thump. "I know someone who would be perfect. She's new to the city but she's a mad dog woman like you, Odie. Want me to call her?"

I looked at Crystal and she shrugged. "You can call her and ask her if she'd like to send a résumé, but tell her that we're pretty early in the hiring process."

In a blur, Shereen had her cellphone in her hand and she was talking loudly. "Tiff! Good news, a job just opened up at the Rescue. I need you to send me your résumé. I'll pass it on to the boss lady herself. Hurry up!"

She tapped her phone after a second and clapped her hands together. "She's super excited. I'll keep my email open so I can forward you her résumé when it pops up. Now that the hiring process is underway, I think you should call Josh."

"No."

That was easier than I expected it to be—saying no, that is. Why was I so desperate to please people again?

"Why not? Once you hire Tiffany, I'll help you get her up to speed. We'll be working like a well-oiled machine before you know it, and voilà, you have time for a relationship. If not a relationship, then a chance to see where things might go."

If I hadn't been so focused on holding my position, I would have laughed at how Shereen just so casually assumed I would hire her friend. "No."

"Think how happy it would make your granny. Just give him a call, see what happens."

"NO."

"Why not?"

"Because if I hadn't been swept up with him, I might have found the money to give Crystal a raise and been paying closer attention to my grandmother, and she might have avoided a hospital visit!"

Crystal swallowed hard and Shereen nodded. "Okay, good, keep talking. Why do you think you could have prevented your grandmother from getting pneumonia?"

"Because if I had been spending time with her, if I had gone to help her with her gardening instead of letting Josh talk me out of it, I would have seen the signs. I would have made her go to the doctor sooner, and she wouldn't have ended up in the hospital! But I was running around with Josh like a silly teenager with her first boyfriend!"

"Did the doctor say how your grandmother got pneumonia?"

"He said she's been doing too much lately. He wants her to scale back on her activities. I had to talk her into giving up on her backyard garden yesterday and it half killed me. I've never known my grandmother without a big backyard full of flowers."

"But did he say how she actually got pneumonia?"

"No…"

"If he didn't say what caused the pneumonia, then why are you harboring so much guilt? If he didn't say for sure what caused it, why are you so certain that you could have prevented it?"

I paused. Shereen was really batting a thousand with the therapy type questions. The more answers I gave, the more I realized how silly I sounded. That wasn't a great feeling, but I didn't mind the feeling of guilt slipping away.

"I guess I couldn't have done anything to prevent it. But I'm not ready to talk to Josh again. Not yet. I was really dismissive with him at the hospital."

"What happened?" Crystal chimed in, her eyes full of vivid interest.

"I didn't see him with you in Granny's room—where was he?" Shereen asked, excitement edging through the therapist-calm tone of her voice.

"We, uh…were together when I got the call from the hospital. He had to take me to her."

"Right, because you were in his car when I took the dogs home for you," Crystal wondered aloud with a knowing smile spreading across her face.

Shereen dropped the coolness entirely. She was spinning around in her swivel chair, clapping and stomping her feet.

"So you guys had a lot of fun, then?" Crystal asked with a really insufferable smile on her face.

"Well, we had cracked open a bottle of wine, we had the dogs hanging around, he was teaching me to fly drones. We were having an okay time."

"Don't be coy, you've pretty much found the man of your dreams!" Shereen gushed. But then she paused. "So if you had so much fun with him, why won't you call him?"

"He took me to the hospital, he got me coffee, and he was really sweet, but then I told him to move on and leave me alone."

"You didn't," Crystal and Shereen said in chorus.

"I did. I was under a lot of stress, things were moving really fast, and I had a bunch of guilt around my grandmother's health. I was kind of an ass."

"I'm sure he would understand. You should call him."

"I don't really know if I should. You didn't see the wounded look on his face when I sent him on his way."

Shereen surprised me by folding her arms across her chest. "Fine, don't call him. I know it will work out in the end. True love always finds a way."

Then she shocked Crystal by swiping a donut out of the box and taking a giant bite. After a second she groaned, "Damn, these are good. I tried to quit you, carbs, but I couldn't. It's like I said, true love always finds a way."

I sat there in stunned silence for a few seconds before sighing and pulling out my phone. Crystal started clapping and I got up and went outside. I dialed Josh's number and listened to it ring and ring. Finally, it went to voicemail.

"You have reached the mailbox of...Joshua Bowen... Please leave a message after the tone."

The phone beeped and I started talking. "Uh, hi Josh.

This is Odie. I wanted to say hi, and tell you that Granny's due to get out of the hospital tonight, so she's, uh, doing really good. I also wanted to say that I'm sorry if I came across as a little distant at the hospital. You were really great to me and I was kind of a shrew. Yeah, I'm really sorry about that. Um, take care."

I ended the call and cringed. Could I have sounded any more like an idiot? But I'd called him, and I said I was sorry. The ball was in his court now. I went back inside and Crystal and Shereen stopped what they were doing.

"So how'd it go?" Crystal asked.

"I got his voicemail."

"Did you leave a message?"

"Yeah. I mean, it would have been weird if I called and didn't leave a message or anything, right?"

"Right. So don't you feel better?"

"Not really. I think I made a fool of myself."

"I'm sure you didn't."

"I know I did. I sounded like a total airhead. But it doesn't matter, I left the voicemail; I said I was sorry, and now the ball's in his court."

Shereen and Crystal shared a look, but Shereen recovered first. "Oh, goody, Tiffany's résumé just popped up. You're going to love her, Odie."

Chapter 24

JOSH

I let Odie's call go to voicemail. It was the day of our meeting with Isaac Archambault and, as curious as I was to hear what she had to say, I couldn't lose focus now.

"Have you heard anything from—?" Victor asked, almost reading my mind, as we drove from his apartment.

"I'd rather not talk about it right now. Can we just listen to some hair metal and try to get pumped up for the meeting?" I said, cutting him off.

"Hair metal? We didn't do that last time."

"And see how well that meeting went? Let's try it. I need the distraction."

Victor found the most awful eighties music station on the radio and we were quiet for the rest of the trip. We got to the office of Archambault Ventures in Brentwood, really not very far from my house, and were welcomed inside by the congenial secretary I'd spoken to on the phone a couple weeks ago. She was middle-aged but to hear her talk, she was more knowledgeable about technology trends than Victor and me combined.

The place was night and day from Doussen and

Associates. Where the other one screamed cold modernity, this one was all warmth and the promise of a better tomorrow. The coffee was proudly labeled as fair trade organic and the cups were compostable. There were brochures for a number of different charities in the waiting room, and I found myself looking to see if Purse Dog Rescue was featured anywhere. I made myself stop; I couldn't get caught up in personal issues right then.

People came trickling in through the office while we waited. Each one greeted us with such earnest politeness that it almost made me wonder what my dad had to do with a nice company like this.

Fifteen minutes passed and the secretary came over and led us to the conference room. "Mr. Archambault is ready to see you now."

We walked into a large conference room and I heard Victor inhale sharply. I looked around and saw Naomi sitting near the head of the table. She smiled at us both but didn't get up to address us. It was probably for the better. Mr. Archambault came around and shook our hands.

"It's a real pleasure to see you two again. Kendall had a lot of great things to say about your project. I thought he was just being partial to his own son's work until I saw the prospectus you sent over. I'm very excited to see your presentation."

I smiled and thanked him for taking the time to see us, but Victor went a step further and said, "Thank you very much, we hope our pitch lives up to your expectations. However, in the interest of full disclosure, we should probably remind you that at one point Naomi Klein was once a good friend of ours."

Isaac's eyes flickered over to Naomi and back to us. "Yes, right, I remember something unusual at the gala. If it would make you more comfortable, we can ask Naomi to sit this meeting out."

I could feel him watching us as Victor and I looked at each other. We didn't feel comfortable discussing the merits of our options, so we settled on subtle head bobs and shakes before I shrugged. "We were friends but it's all ancient history. After the gala, I think we're all caught up."

"Excellent. We'll get started in just a few minutes, then."

Mr. Archambault wandered off and Victor and I got busy setting up our materials and presentation. Once everyone was seated, we looked at Mr. Archambault and he nodded once, smiling.

I cleared my throat and said, "Thank you for coming here today to hear our talk…"

———

We walked out of the conference room not knowing quite what to think. They'd let us finish and then asked some really good questions at the end, which we handled pretty well between us.

"Victor, Josh! Do you have a moment?" Mr. Archambault called from behind us as we reached the door of the building.

Victor recovered first. "Of course."

"We want to fund the Nacho-Copter. We know this isn't standard behavior for venture capital companies, but we're sure that your subscription-based business model will make the difference. Our attorneys need some time to put together the paperwork, but we'll be in touch in the next day or two to have you come in to go over the paperwork and our offer. If you're interested in going forward, that is?"

I looked at Victor and he had a huge smile on his face as he said, "Yes, I suppose we are. Is there anything you need from us right now?"

"Not at the moment, but we'll be in touch if we do."

He shook our hands one more time, and Victor and I walked out of the building before losing our minds in the parking lot.

"Holy shit! We did it!" Victor whooped.

"I know. Shit, what do we do?"

"Call everyone we know? Go to Vegas and see if our luck holds?"

My shoulders sank as I had a thought. "We should probably call my dad first."

Victor nodded and started putting things in the back of the trunk. I went around to the driver's seat and called my dad.

"Kendall Bowen speaking."

"Hi Dad. We just got out of the meeting with Isaac Archambault and we wanted to tell you how it went."

"Well, how'd it go?"

"We got it. We're getting funded."

He laughed. "That's excellent. I knew he would be a good fit for you, even if he doesn't normally go in for products like yours. I'm proud of you two. Lana's out shopping, but supposedly she'll be home soon. Once we're together, we can decide how to celebrate."

"Thanks, Dad."

The call ended and Victor slid into the passenger seat. "So how'd that go?"

"Pretty well. He wants us to do something to celebrate."

"Think he'll be on board for a Brazilian steakhouse?"

"We can ask."

We started driving and Victor turned to me. "So

Naomi didn't try to talk to either of us. How do you feel about that?"

"I don't really. She really is ancient history."

He smiled. "Glad to hear it. So now that the Nacho-Copter's funded, are you going to check in with Odie?"

I remembered her call from earlier in the morning and almost pulled my phone out of my pocket. Why not test my luck a little more?

When we stopped at a light, I turned to Victor. "Do you remember that comment you made when Odie helped us with the presentation?"

"About the two grand donation to the Rescue? I haven't forgotten. We can go by a print shop and get one of those giant checks if you're looking to make some kind of grand gesture."

"That's not necessary. I'll drop you at home, but I want you to call the office and make the donation, okay?"

"Whatever you say. I'll be your best man if you ask nicely."

"Shut up."

I didn't want to get my hopes up.

Chapter 25

ODIE

Right as I walked into the office, my phone chimed with a reminder. I glanced at the screen and smacked my forehead. Granny's birthday was today! How could I have forgotten? I was a terrible granddaughter. First, I neglected to notice she was coming down with pneumonia and now I didn't have a gift or anything.

I must have been grumbling pretty loudly to myself because Crystal rolled over to my desk and started patting my head.

"What? You've been whining for like a solid five minutes."

I batted her hand away and tried to smooth the frizzy hair around my temples. "I forgot about Granny's birthday. I don't have time to shop; I need to follow up with some people from the gala and start going through applications for your successor."

"All of that can wait, just go now and pick something up. You'll be so much more productive if you take care of it instead of wallowing in guilt."

Shereen came to lean on my desk. "You know, you

could just hire Tiffany and cross that second activity off your list. Also, I have an idea for a gift for your grandmother."

Tiffany's résumé was pretty spectacular. I had already arranged a phone interview but I wasn't going to tell Shereen that. I was through with people-pleasing. "I'm still thinking about it. But what's your idea for Granny's gift?"

"Make a kit for her to start a container garden. Her doctor wanted her to slow down. One pot of flowers requires a lot less work than a full backyard."

Crystal nodded. "Yeah, you could stop by a gardening store or something, pick up a nice planter and some soil. I don't know if I'd buy a plant, though. She'd probably rather pick that out herself. But then you'd have at least something to give her."

She was onto something there. Before I could reply, my phone started ringing. I pulled it out of my desk drawer. Lana Bowen was calling me, and I couldn't imagine why.

"Hello?"

"Odie, darling, this is Lana, Diego's foster." I must have squeaked because she hastened to say, "He's fine, but I wanted to talk to you about your granny."

I sat back in my chair. "Yes, she's determined to be at Bible study this week. She was furious that I made her sit it out last week. Do you think you could maybe talk the other ladies into meeting at her house this week?"

"I'm sure I could work something out. Anyway, I wanted to talk to you about her birthday. I know it's been a rough couple of weeks for you two, so I thought I'd take care of dinner. What do you think?"

"Oh, that's really kind of you. We wouldn't want to put you to any trouble."

"Darling, it's no trouble at all. I was just thinking of something small—we could do dinner at her house if you think that would be easier on her. Mary Agatha's one of the finest women I've ever met and I think she deserves a good birthday. What time should I come with dinner?"

"Umm...for tonight?"

"Yes, unless you made other plans."

"Oh, that's really thoughtful of you..." I struggled to think of an appropriate response. Granny's house wasn't at all ready for company, but if I suggested that we do dinner tomorrow, it might look like I had nothing special planned. But what the hell. "Any time after eight is fine."

"I'll be there at eight fifteen. Would you mind if I brought Josh along? I know he's been worried about your grandmother."

I felt a stab of guilt. "Oh, yes, that would be fine."

"That's wonderful, dear. Well, I'm going to let you go; I'm sure there's plenty to do at the Rescue. Speaking of which, could you bring the adoption papers for Diego to your grandmother's house tonight? I've been doing a lot of thinking and I just can't stand the thought of giving him up. You know what that's like, right?"

I didn't have to force a smile for the telephone there. "Granny's probably told you stories about my dogs, you know I understand. I'm so excited for you and Diego. I'll see you tonight with the adoption papers."

"Until then, darling."

The line went dead and I looked at Crystal. She saw my wide eyes and seemed to almost start panicking herself. "What? That didn't sound bad, but you have this look on your face like something terrible happened. What?"

I got up and started digging around the filing cabinets that lined the wall behind my desk for copies of our adoption papers. "That was Lana, Josh's stepmother. She wants to bring a birthday dinner to Granny's house tonight. But that's not all. She asked to bring Josh to visit. On top of all that, she wants to start the adoption process for Diego. Isn't that just great?"

Shereen whooped. "That's amazing! I'm so happy for you! This is really a good day for you: Granny's fine, Diego's getting a forever home, and you're getting another chance with Josh. I could just sing for happiness."

Crystal tilted her head at Shereen as if to say that she had a point, without actually using the words. I finally found the adoption papers and started filling them out with Diego's information. When the office got quiet, Crystal came to sit next to me.

"It's going to be okay. I'll come with you to keep things from getting awkward. Stop grinding your teeth."

I pulled a stress ball out of my desk and squeezed it until we closed the Rescue for the day. Before we headed to Granny's, Shereen gave us each a hug and told us to wish her a happy birthday. We stopped at a garden store before going to Granny's house. When we pulled up to the curb, Josh's car was parked in the driveway. I took a deep breath and hauled Granny's present to the door. Crystal rang the doorbell and we were greeted by Zsa Zsa and Granny.

"Happy birthday!" Crystal and I said in unison.

Granny smiled. "Thank you. What do you have there in your arms?"

"Your birthday present. I was thinking we could start your container garden with this."

"That's too sweet of you. Come in; Lana and Josh are already here and you would not believe how much food they brought. You should call Shereen and see if she wants to come over. No, Zsa Zsa, you can't go outside. Crystal, will you make sure the cat doesn't make a break for it, please?"

We followed Granny into the kitchen where Lana was

sitting with a glass of wine. Plates covered the kitchen table and I saw why Granny wanted more people to help eat it.

Lana watched our reactions and grinned. "Who's hungry?"

There was a snort and I saw Josh standing off to the side, near the phone nook. Crystal decided to introduce herself to Lana.

I went over to Josh and said, "Hi."

"Hi."

Awkward. What was I supposed to do? The ball was in his court—I'd called him back. He hadn't called me back, but now I was supposed to carry the conversation?

As if he had read my mind, he said, "Sorry I didn't return your call earlier. I was just about to go into my meeting with Archambault."

My eyes widened. "How'd it go?"

"Victor should be calling with his donation soon if he hasn't already. But it went great, we got the funding we needed from him. Thanks to you, of course. He was a huge fan of the business model you suggested to us."

"You're too kind. You would have thought of it too. I didn't sell it, either, that was all you and Victor."

Lana got up and offered us each a glass of wine and gestured at the table. "Eat something, please; our cook really knocked it out of the park today. I told her this was for Diego's benefactors and she was on it. Really, though, you have to try the brisket. Now, Odie, I don't want to rush you, but I was wondering—"

Josh took a glass from his stepmother and walked over to the table. I couldn't stop a sigh and turned my attention to Lana. "I have the adoption papers in my bag. I already filled out most of it for you."

"That's great to hear, but I was also wondering—"

Lana let her voice drop "—should I not have brought Josh? I didn't mean for things to be awkward for you."

I cleared my throat. It was awkward, but it was Granny's birthday and I didn't want to make it about my drama. So I shook my head. "No, we're fine. It's just been a strange couple of days. But we're fine."

"That's wonderful, because he was so happy once you two started hanging out. Losing Esperanza was hard on him, and Kendall and I have just about tried everything to get him to cheer up. You don't know how special you are to him."

Not quite sure how to react to that, I shrugged. "I'm sure you're giving me too much credit. But tonight should be about Granny, she's had a rough couple of weeks."

Lana squeezed my arm and went over to talk to Granny and Crystal. I went over to the table and started piling food on my plate.

"What do you think of the wine?" Josh surprised me by asking.

"It's pretty good, not as a good as the wine we had at the beach house, though." I smiled at the thought of the ridiculous wine cellar.

"Would you like to try that again sometime?" He asked in one rushed breath and raised his glass to his lips.

The sight of his full lips reminded me of all the fun we'd had. I missed him, but I just wasn't sure how to say as much. I shifted my weight from one foot to the other and said, "Once my grandmother's doing better and I have Crystal's successor trained, definitely. But in the meantime, would you like to get coffee again?"

He leaned forward and kissed me on the cheek. "Name the day."

I could feel myself burning up, and then Granny

decided to say, "We should have set these two up years ago. What were we waiting for anyway, Lana?"

There was no mistaking Crystal's snort, and Lana sighed. "Mary Agatha, you just got out of the hospital, and I don't want to send you back there with the truth, but I think they fell in love despite our best matchmaking efforts."

Love? Who said anything about love? I looked at Josh and he whispered in my ear, "They're just trying to get a reaction out of us. I'm not trying to push you into anything you're not ready for, I promise."

"Careful now, I'll hold you to it," I whispered back.

"I wouldn't have it any other way, angel."

Chapter 26

JOSH

I had been planning my proposal for a month and it was all going to be a disaster if I couldn't get Woz to cooperate.

Odie was on her way home from work and I had everything set up perfectly at her house—well, our house. She'd asked me to move in a few months ago and it took a little while for Ceviche and me to adjust to four dogs. Most of Odie's dogs were fine with us, but Woz was the main holdout. His problem wasn't even with Ceviche—those two were best buds—it was mostly a problem with me. But I needed Woz's help tonight.

He grumbled at me when I picked him up. I was probably going to find a present in my shoes tomorrow, but I was laser-focused on tying a note and a silicone ring to his collar. When I set him down, he tried to bite at the ring and note but he didn't manage to untie them. That was good enough for me. I patted the ring box in my pocket. The silicone rings were a nice suggestion from Lana. Ceviche and all four of Odie's dogs had decoy rings tied to their collars, and if everything went to plan, they were going to lead Odie back to the living room where I would be waiting with a bouquet of flowers and the real ring.

I didn't hear her pull into the driveway but I did hear the door slam. She was talking on her phone when she came inside.

"Tiffany, you are a genius. You got every single person I talked to at the gala to donate or fundraise for Purse Dog! You and Shereen have fun clubbing tonight. I'm going to…call you back later…bye."

From where I was standing in the living room, I saw her kneel down and pick up Woz.

"What's this, buddy?" Odie said, removing the note and the ring from his collar. She stared at them for a while.

I knew Woz was going to screw this up. I bit my lip and waited to see what she would do next.

"Josh?" she called, throwing her purse down on the kitchen counter.

"Back here in the living room," I said, only hesitating for a moment.

She made it to the threshold and froze. I held the bouquet of roses in my hand and smiled. "Hi angel."

I watched her swallow. "Woz had something around his neck."

"Weird, right? You should check the other dogs too."

Her eyebrows rose. "Oh?"

"Yeah, it's the strangest thing; I think Ceviche has something too."

When Odie whistled for the dogs and they all came running, I finally remembered to breathe. At least one thing was going as planned.

She held up all of the notes from the dogs and after a minute started reading them aloud. "'Will you marry me?'"

That wasn't at all how I'd planned on her reading that.

But I rolled with it. "Why, yes, I will. I think I even have a ring."

She laughed and I stood next to her. I dropped the bouquet on the coffee table and wrapped my arms around her.

"Odessa Jane Ferguson, will you please marry me?"

I felt her tense and my stomach began to sink. Maybe I read the signs wrong. I almost let her go just as she said, "Yes. But am I supposed to wear like all five silicone rings?"

The relief I felt was indescribable. I kissed her and only spoke when we broke apart for air. "You can but I also have something else you could try on instead."

I pulled the ring box out of my pocket and Odie gasped. Mary Agatha had told me Odie would probably love my mother's engagement ring, and judging by the tear slipping down her cheek, she was right.

"Do you want to try it on?" I said, pulling the ring out of the box.

Odie swallowed and I slid the ring on her left hand. In the light of the living room, the oval shaped diamond caught the light and sparkled alongside the emerald baguettes. It was a fit.

I gave her another kiss and held her hand in mine as I asked, "Would you like to call people now or should we have dinner first?"

"Dinner. Definitely dinner."

"Excellent, I have pizza coming in…" I glanced at my watch. "…ten minutes or so and champagne in the fridge. But more importantly, do you like the ring?"

She looked down at the ring and up at me and said, "Well, it's a nice ring, but it's not a Chihuahua."

"I figured you already had four."

"Dogs are a girl's best friend, not diamonds. Haven't you heard?"

"Come here and we'll get you as many dogs as you want in the morning."

That was the perfect thing to say. Odie pulled me into a kiss; we fell on the couch and made out until the dogs started barking like mad. I wiped lipgloss off my lips and found the pizza guy waiting at the door.

He handed me the boxes and smirked at me. "Good night?"

"The greatest," I said, signing the receipt and closing the door before Woz could go all Cujo on him.

"What'd you get?" Odie asked as she walked into the kitchen.

I shielded the pizza boxes from her view. "Well, I wasn't sure what your answer would be, so I decided to hedge my bets. A wise woman once told me that 'true love conquers all,' so there was really only one pizza I could get. Sit down and let me get you a drink."

She giggled and sat at the kitchen table. I popped open the champagne and poured two glasses. I handed her one and then opened the top pizza box.

Odie sat up in her seat to see what was inside. "Meat-lovers! You really are too corny."

"No, I'm romantic."

I couldn't keep a straight face. We laughed, kissed, and stuffed our faces with pizza. I even rewarded Woz for his participation in the night's events with a bite of pizza crust.

Epilogue

ODIE

Granny and Lana wasted no time planning our wedding. I'd tried to stay out of the way—I had so much to do. Tiffany just kept raking in the grant money, so Purse Dog Rescue was in the middle of a huge expansion, and Josh was so busy with the Nacho-Copter, we were happy to spend our time together doing anything but wedding preparation. I showed up for dress fittings and cake tasting, and answered texts about my preferences for roses versus peonies, but I staunchly refused to weigh in on favors. They were just such a waste when we could tell everyone we had donated the money to animals in need anyway. But Granny and Lana thought that was tacky. So Josh took it up with Kendall and managed to get them to agree instead to giving a donation to a selection of well-regarded charities in the name of the guests who had RSVP'd.

I peeked out of the window from one of the twenty guest rooms in the Bowen mansion. My room was facing the gardens and I could see the tent where the reception would be held gleaming white in the Southern California sun. It was a beautiful day for a garden ceremony and I was getting more excited by the minute.

"Don't walk backward! You'll trip on the train and break your neck!" Crystal scolded as she rushed behind me to straighten my train.

"Fine, I'll stick to moving forward. Maybe I should have gone with Granny and Lana to pick out the dress…" I said as I stared down at the voluminous mass of taffeta and tulle. It was pretty, but I just wasn't sure if it was right for an outdoor wedding where dogs featured prominently in the wedding party.

Crystal was all business. Her new job and her part-time law school classes had turned her into a fiend for efficiency. "Too late for that. Let's get going. We don't want to rush down the stairs."

"The guests aren't even supposed to be here for another half hour. Besides, isn't the photographer supposed to meet us soon to take pictures of us?"

"Ha, I forgot. Fine. I'll go find the photographer. Do not sit down!"

"But these shoes pinch," I whined.

Crystal rolled her eyes and pointed a finger at Shereen. "She doesn't sit. Hold her upright if you have to. That dress cannot be wrinkled before the wedding!"

Shereen was applying a thick gloss to her baby-pink lips, and made a sort of tongue click to acknowledge Crystal's command. Right there I saw who should have been my maid of honor. Crystal marched off in her long pink-and-white maxi dress and Shereen got up to stand next to me.

"Have you seen Josh today?"

"No, he's been banished to the pool house on Lana's orders. I think Kendall's having fun with all the traditions too."

"Do you mind that he's walking you down the aisle?"

"No, it works out nicely. My dad's not around to do it, and Kendall never got a chance to do it for his daughter."

"The ceremony isn't going to include anything about giving anybody away, is it?"

"Are you kidding? Granny made it very clear that I wasn't going to be passed over like chattel."

"Right on, Granny. What's going on down there?"

We craned our necks to see Tiffany, who had been roped into playing wedding coordinator for the day, chasing after a blur that looked a lot like Carmencita. The blur was running toward the tent but came to a screeching halt in front of a familiar silhouette.

"That's Victor, right?" Shereen asked, fanning herself in the nonexistent heat.

"Looks like it," I said as we watched Tiffany come to a stop in front of Victor. Even from two stories up, it was obvious she was blushing beet red. "He does have a knack for playing Carmencita's champion."

We watched Victor and Tiffany awkwardly dance around each other for a few minutes until Crystal returned with the photographer and Granny.

"Odie, we're going to need you to turn slowly," Crystal said. "Hold her hand, Shereen, so she doesn't lose her balance. We're going to walk part of the way downstairs where you'll take your solo pictures. Let's try to make this quick."

Granny came up to me and squeezed my arm. "You look better than Grace Kelly. You can thank me after the wedding…by maybe naming one of your daughters Mary Agatha?"

"You saying things like that just makes me more inclined to name one of my imaginary children Zsa Zsa." I hugged her anyway.

I stole one last glance at Victor and Tiffany before Shereen took my hand and spun me around. Granny and I giggled but Crystal was considerably less amused.

"Are you trying to kill her, Shereen? Be careful!"

I picked up my skirts and followed them and the photographer down the hallway. Right as I started walking down the staircase, Josh came bounding up the steps.

"Cover your eyes! You can't see her yet!" Crystal yelled as she stood in front of him, trying to block him from seeing me.

"He's seen me naked before, I don't think the tradition means much if we've already consummated the relationship!" I cried in exasperation.

"Sorry, sorry. I just, I need to get my tie pin. It was a present from Esperanza and I want to have it for the wedding."

The photographer nodded. "Go get it and come back. We'll just do both of your pictures together while we have you here."

Josh turned to me, even with Crystal hitting him, and I said, "Yes, I love that idea. Let's get as many pictures out of the way as we can."

Crystal groaned but Shereen elbowed her. "True love always finds a way. You can plan and plan, but sometimes things work out even better."

I turned to Josh and he was laughing. "Shereen might have a better toast ready than Victor."

He pulled me into a kiss and when we broke apart I whispered, "Victor had better watch out, Carmencita's been trying to play Cupid again."

Acknowledgments

There are enough people who deserve my thanks that this acknowledgement section could be a whole book on its own. First thanks need to go to my editors, Serena Clarke and Michelle Leedy, it was a privilege to work with you. Right up there with the editors is Jake. I probably couldn't have finished writing a romance novel without experiencing the love and happiness of our marriage. Many thanks also to Juliet, my cousin and best friend, for listening to me talk about story ideas and writing projects for ages.

To my writing friends in Virginia: Kate Flegal, Lisa Schwartz, Amanda Massey and Jeffrey C. Jacobs, I wouldn't be half the writer I am today without your help. For helping me put the crowning touches on this story and giving me the courage to put this story out there for the world to see, I thank my fellow members of San Antonio Romance Authors, particularly Mary Brand, Willa Blair, Tara West, and Maida Malby. If I left anyone out, please know I am eternally grateful for your help in taking this book from idea to happily ever after.

About the Author

Erin L Jungdahl (yeah, you read that right "Young-dahl") wrote a story about cats and dogs the moment she figured out how to write. She went on to write about princesses, mermaids, robots, and spies. Erin lives in San Antonio with her husband and three cats. She is back to writing about cats and dogs and loving every minute of it. Connect with her at erinljungdahlbooks.com today.

facebook.com/ErinJungdahl

twitter.com/erinljungdahl

instagram.com/erinljungdahl

bookbub.com/authors/erinljungdahl

pinterest.com/erinljungdahl

goodreads.com/ErinLJungdahl

Mata Hari Squad

Nothing can stop a spy on a mission, except maybe one of her partners.

Miranda Watson wants two things in life: a good bottle of wine and a promotion. Not at her day job, her real job: espionage. The work makes her feel alive but her newest partner is killing her... chances for that coveted promotion.

When she uncovers a contractor blackmailing a politician, Miranda is certain that she's found her ticket to the top. Her partner has loftier concerns. Can they set aside their differences to save a woman's life?

Mata Hari Squad is a spy novel for people looking for Jane Bond.

If you like James Bond, Scandal, and Charlie's Angels, you should check this story out today!

Coming Soon

Meet Cute Chihuahua: a Romantic Comedy

Tiffany didn't come to California looking for love. She actually climbed out of a church window to avoid getting married. Her life was complete with an adorable rescue dog, a job helping animals, and amazing friends. Then a renegade Chihuahua led her to the most handsome man she'd ever seen.

This was the second time Victor stopped a rampaging Chihuahua but he wasn't complaining. Tiffany was just the kind of woman he'd been waiting for. Their attraction was immediate and yet their courtship was a comedy of errors.

If you like stories of peoples and dogs finding forever families and plenty of laughter, you'll love Meet Cute Chihuahua.